CARSON'S REVENGE

When the Mexican bandit General Rodriguez hangs Carson's grandfather, the youngster vows revenge, and with that aim joins the Texas Rangers. Then as Carson escorts Mexican Henrietta Xavier to her home, Rodriguez kidnaps her. The ranger plucks the heiress from the general's clutches, and the youngsters make a desperate run for the border and safety. Will Carson's strength and courage be enough to save them as he tries to get the better of the brutal general and his bandits?

JIM WILSON

CARSON'S REVENGE

Complete and Unabridged

LINFORD
Leicester

First published in Great Britain in 2007 by
Robert Hale Limited
London

First Linford Edition
published 2008
by arrangement with
Robert Hale Limited
London

British Library CIP Data

Wilson, Jim (Jim C.)
Carson's revenge.—Large print ed.—
Linford western library
1. Western stories
2. Large type books
I. Title
823.9′2 [F]

ISBN 978–1–84782–244–4

Published by
F. A. Thorpe (Publishing)
Anstey, Leicestershire

Set by Words & Graphics Ltd.
Anstey, Leicestershire
Printed and bound in Great Britain by
T. J. International Ltd., Padstow, Cornwall

1

General Rodriguez sat on his big Spanish stallion and looked through the glasses at the peaceful village scene. There were very few people about at that time of the day. Most were either working or partaking of midday meals. The village looked almost deserted. Then he saw the people sitting outside the cantina under a canvas awning. There were a good dozen or so scattered about the wooden tables drinking or eating.

'Sergio, are the men in position?'

Sergio a tall, lean, rugged looking man with a grey peppered moustache, nodded without turning his head. Rodriguez checked his watch. It was generally unreliable but he thought it gave him a touch of class.

'Another five minutes, then.'

Sergio nodded again.

'Yes, General.'

The raid was simple. Rodriguez's men surrounded a particular village inside Texas and well away from the Mexican border. Once the area was cordoned off the bandits then swept through the dwellings killing anyone who offered resistance and taking captive those suitable for selling on as slaves. The villages were usually too poor to offer much in the way of valuables so slaves were taken instead.

Desperate parents and relatives offered bribes to the bandits to pass on to the next house and allow a brother or father or husband or son their liberty. Sometimes they were successful. Often the bribe they could afford was not enough or the bandits were afraid of being caught by Rodriguez and punished for accepting bribes.

The wily ones pocketed the payment and moved on leaving the relieved families to hang on to their loved ones. On the fateful day that was to change Carson's destiny the bandits were raiding Perdue, his home village.

Engrossed in their work inside the forge neither Carson nor his grandfather was aware of the disturbance as the bandits swept into the village. The first indication that something was amiss was a violent hammering upon the forge doors. As they turned from their work at the smouldering furnace four armed bandits burst into the forge.

The men peered into the smoky interior. This was a prize indeed — two strong men — one young, one old but still looking hardy enough for work in the mines. A burly brigand used the butt of his carbine to prod Carson.

'Outside!'

Carson backed up. The bandits were motioning with their weapons.

'Get out of my smithy!'

The roar of his grandfather's voice filled the interior of the workshop.

The sergeant swung his rifle and caught the old man across the side of the head. The big man staggered back, almost overbalancing on to the forge.

He shook his large shaggy head. Blood welled from a cut and seeped into his grey-white hair.

The growl of anger was low and guttural as he swung the tongs still grasped in his hand. But the bandit blocked the tongs with his weapon and swung the rifle once more.

The tongs wielded by the old man in turn blocked the rifle and a hammer in the other hand smashed into the bandit's face. The stricken man dropped to his knees. The hammer rose and fell again. This time the hammer cracked on top of the bandit's head.

The insensible body pitched forward to the floor and twitched for a few awful moments while the life functions carried on as if unaware of their driver's sudden demise. The man's companions were staring in consternation at the body stretched out on the floor of the smithy.

Carson's grandad blinked blood from his eyes. He looked at the dead bandit lying in front of the forge belatedly realizing what he had done. Slowly he dropped to his knees and regarded his gruesome handiwork. Carson moved to stand beside him staring at the blood leaking from the dead man on to the earthen floor. The lethal hammer dangled loosely from his grandfather's fingers.

'Gramps, are you OK?'

The smithy looked up at his grandson. He realized the implications of what had happened before the younger man. As he began to speak his grandson was struck violently on the back of the head and pitched forward on top of the old man. The bandits crowded forward raining blows upon the two men. When they stepped back the battered smithies had joined the dead bandit on the forge floor.

'Get them outside.'

Hands grasped Carson's boots and dragged him into the street. He slid and bumped through the doorway barely conscious of his surroundings. The bandits went back for the old man.

Carson struggled to make his body function. As he lay semi-conscious he could hear a heated discussion among the bandits as they crowded round, undecided what to do. One of the men put a gun nozzle to the old smith's head and looked questionably at his companions.

'No,' rasped a small, mean-looking man with a long scar down one side of his face. 'Find a rope — we'll have a proper hanging.'

The bandit holding the gun to the old man grinned at Scarface.

'*Sí*, it what this old *bastardo* deserves.'

As the meaning of the man's behaviour sunk in Carson groaned and tried to get up. A brutal blow with a rifle butt drove him back again.

Two of the bandits hurried inside the smithy to rummage about for a rope. The man guarding Carson and his grandfather pushed the gun hard against the old smith's head.

'You hear that, old man. You're going

to dance for us. You're going to dance on the end of a rope.'

The battered smith groaned feebly and tried to sit up. The bandit put his boot on his head and shoved him back.

'Don't move, you old *bastardo*.'

Beside him Carson moved in the dusty street. Blood ran in dark streaks from a gash in his head. Through the pain he looked towards his grandfather.

'Grandad . . . '

He tried to sit up. There was an explosion in his head and once more he lapsed into darkness. The man who had hit him grinned down at the youngster lying in the dirt.

'Hard headed *bastardos* these gringos,' he muttered.

With whoops of delight the two bandits emerged from the smith brandishing a hefty coil of rope.

'We found it. We found a rope.'

The smith's shop was situated in a large three-story building. As well as a smithy the top floors served as a grain store. From partway up the front wall a wooden beam projected out into the roadway. This beam was part of a gantry that supported a pulley and hawser to haul the heavy bags of grain up into the top floors of the warehouse.

It took several throws before the rope curled over the beam. It also took two of the men to drag the old man upright.

Carson was vaguely aware of someone kicking him in the side. The pain in his head pounded continuously like a hammer banging on one of his grandfather's anvils. He tried to sit upright. Agonising pain flared through his head. As he struggled to orient himself he stared around him through pain-filled eyes.

Trying to clear his head he at last managed to focus on the drama before the forge.

'See what happens to gringo *bastardos* that attack General Rodriguez's men.'

The boot slammed into Carson again.

'If you don't obey orders you're next

for a rope collar.'

'Nooo . . . ' he moaned.

This was all part of some nightmare. The pounding agony in his head was excruciating. With a groan of pain and a great deal of effort he managed to struggle to his feet.

'Nooo . . . '

The sight of that grand old man kicking and twisting on the end of a rope was too much to take in. He staggered forward reaching towards the dangling body kicking out its last gasp of breath. The bandits tried to stop him.

With a great cry of rage Carson grabbed the two nearest men. The strength he found came from some deep well of grief and horror — horror at the brutal treatment of the man he loved. That man now dangled in the air, kicking out his life on the end of one of his own ropes. And for what? He had only tried to protect his smith from these invaders.

Carson brought the heads of the men

9

together with such force that the cracking of bone was heard clearly. It was instant and brutal execution and the bandits went limp in his hands. The remaining bandit tried to bring his carbine to bear on the deranged youth. A club-like fist flung him against the side of the building and he slid unconscious to the ground.

Desperately the young apprentice looked around for some means to cut down his grandfather. With a stiletto recovered from one of the dead men he frantically sawed at the rope. It seemed ages before the thick rope parted and he was able to lower his mentor to the ground.

There was no sign of life.

'Please, Grandad. Speak to me.'

Carson rubbed the old man's face and felt for a pulse. Tears coursed down his face and dripped onto the grey hairs of his grandfather. Carson could hardly comprehend this terrible loss. He sobbed out his grief and pain. He was oblivious to all around him. Gathering the old man in his arms he hugged the body to him. Rocking back and forth in the dust of the roadway he sobbed inconsolably.

From behind someone grabbed his shoulder. With a snarl Carson rounded on this new threat. Just before he struck he realized in time it was Jacko, an old friend of his grandfather.

'Carson,' Jacko said urgently, 'get out of here before they find you.'

Carson stared uncomprehendingly at the man.

'They hanged the old man. He's dead. What'll I do?'

Jacko grabbed the youth and bullied him inside the smithy.

'Their friends will come looking and when they realize what has happened they'll hang you too. You've got to go on the run.'

'Where? Where can I go?'

'Go north. Join up with the Texas Rangers. Charlie McNelly will be glad of strong young recruits. Then you'll be able to come back and kill some more of these murdering Mexes. Go quickly before it's too late. I'll look after your grandfather.'

Carson fled the village. He went with only the clothes he stood up in. Charlie McNelly was about to take in another recruit for his ranger companies.

In his heart burned a vengeful resentment for the man he held ultimately responsible for the brutal killing of his grandfather. Looking back towards the faint outline of Perdue, Carson clenched his fists and shook them at the sky.

'I will come for you, Rodriguez. I will learn to fight and come for you. I swear this by the spirit of my grandfather murdered by your thugs. I swear this.'

2

The cavalcade set out from Belido. Though their destination was Del Rio the ranger captain in charge of Henrietta Xavier's safety chose a route that would take them wide of Stockton Plateau. It was round these areas that bandits operated.

Henrietta Xavier was the daughter of a wealthy Mexican rancher, Don Manuel Romero Xavier. Using his wealth and influence he had persuaded McNelly to assign his Texas Rangers to escort his daughter to her home just over the Mexican border.

The girl travelled in a luxurious carriage, her possessions piled on the vehicle's wide roof. Heavily armed riders surrounded the fancy coach while two rangers rode ahead as scouts. The danger of kidnapping was very real.

McNelly did not mind using his men to protect the girl. No one wanted the daughter of such a wealthy and influential rancher to fall into the hands of bandits and become a bargaining piece for ransom.

Among these Texas Rangers riding escort was a giant of a young man on whose saddle was slung a great hammer. His fellow recruits ribbed him unmercifully about this odd weapon.

'You'll be a great help when my boots need mending.'

The young recruit was Carson. He took the banter of his fellow rangers with affable good humour.

Carson at odd moments reflected on the path that had led him to this career as a ranger. His future had been marked out very differently. His ambition had been to work with his blacksmith grandfather in the small village of Perdue.

Well into his sixties, his grandfather had still been able to ply his trade but had yearned to pass on his craft to the younger generation. Carson was to be the recipient of that knowledge. How different his life would have been if the bandits had not come into Perdue that day.

Carson had been a giant among his peers. He had outgrown his brothers and indeed the other children of the locality. When he had reached thirteen summers he was as tall and strong as an eighteen-year old.

'I don't know how we're to keep feeding such a great lummox,' his mother complained. 'I can hardly keep him filled.'

His unusual strength and size had prompted his parents to set him on as an apprentice to the old man.

'Your grandfather is getting more and more work,' his father informed him. 'He needs an apprentice. You can help him with the heavier tasks and then as time goes on you will become skilled in the metal working and become a blacksmith also.'

'It's about time he earned his keep,

anyway,' grumbled his mother. 'He's eating us out of house and home.'

Carson loved the smoky old forge and the eccentric patriarch that ran it. The blacksmith was full of stories about the past. During breaks from the noisier work he would reminisce about the wars he had fought against the Mexicans.

The big man would sit with his pipe adding to the general fog in the workshop and talk. He had massive shoulders and huge arms and hands. It was not hard to see where Carson had inherited his great size.

As he talked the old man would spit from time to time into the fire in the forge. This fire was never allowed to go out. It was one of Carson's tasks to feed this red-hot hungry maw. Daily he poured vast quantities of charcoal into the fire.

The old man would pump the bellows and flames and sparks would fly in to the chimney. Picking up the tongs the smith would grip the white-hot ingot of metal and draw the glowing bar on to the anvil. Then Carson would swing into action. While the smithy held the tongs steady the young man's brawny arms pounded the fiery bar with his heavy hammer.

As early as he could remember that is what had lured him to his grandfather's smithy where he had sat in the smoky, dim inferno, soaking in the sensations that would live in his memories. The sound of a hammer on anvil — the hissing of water turning into steam as the cherry coloured iron was plunged into the tub of water — the roar of the flames through the charcoal as the bellows pumped the air into the fire — the smell of the wet steam — these were his childhood memories. It was his favourite daydream.

As Carson rode escort for the young Mexican aristocrat he relived that last fateful day of his apprenticeship. The pain was still there, as was the desire for revenge.

The scouts saw the wagon slewed

across the road. They reported back to their captain.

'They're just peons, sir. Got a wheel off.'

'Very well,' grumbled the captain, a balding man of medium build notorious for strict discipline and procedure.

He climbed nimbly from his horse and walked forward. The men surrounding the broken down vehicle were dressed in ragged clothes and were engaged in some sort of argument. The captain marched stiffly towards the wagon blocking the roadway.

'Damned sloppy Mexicans,' he muttered. 'Can't fix a goddamn wheel.'

He arrived at the barrier.

'Get this wagon moved. We need to come through.'

The men who turned to stare at the captain were hard faced Mexicans. The looks they gave the ranger were distinctly unfriendly. A stream of Spanish followed. The captain looked disgusted.

'Damn you, clear the road and let my convoy through.'

Again he was faced with a barrage of incomprehensible Spanish. He turned and yelled back to the men awaiting his orders.

'Some of you men come up here and help these greasers with this wagon.'

Men were beginning to dismount.

'That won't be necessary, senor.'

The captain looked down at the revolver in the Mexican's hand.

'What the hell . . . '

As well as being a stickler for discipline and order the captain was a man of action and brave as well. Wheeling around he shouted a warning to his men. The revolver smashed into the back of his head and he collapsed on the roadway.

Suddenly around the coach and its escort armed men appeared from out of hiding. They flourished guns and snarled instructions for the rangers to dismount. The ranger company was completely taken by surprise. They looked uneasily at the weapons pointed at them and reluctantly conceded defeat.

3

The ambush had been cleverly sited. The convoy had been stopped along a road flanked by large cactus plants giving good cover for the lurking bandits. The peons the captain had considered useless were now suddenly armed and dangerous. Everything had happened so quickly the rangers were taken unawares and disarmed without incident.

Carson had started forward with his hammer, thinking to be of use in repairing the broken down wagon. He was caught between the two forces and was being ignored for the moment. He peered up the road to where Henrietta Xavier was being escorted from the coach.

A powerfully built figure in a military uniform stepped forward to greet Henrietta. The young ranger could see the girl was greatly agitated. She looked tiny beside the bulk of the man. Carson wondered briefly who he was.

Suddenly the girl swung her fist and punched the man as he bowed to her. The uniformed man did not seem bothered by this. He reached up and grabbed her wrists. She struggled against him. Seeing the girl struggling with the big man prompted Carson to act.

In front of him was one of the armed bandits. The man's attention was fixed on the drama being enacted up beside the coach. Carson wrapped a sturdy arm around the Mexican's neck. At the same time he hit him on the temple with his clenched fist. A second blow punched the bandit into unconsciousness.

Carson plucked the carbine from the unconscious man's slack grip as he slumped to the ground and turning quickly, plunged into the cacti bordering the road. There were shouts behind him and shots were fired. He ignored the gunshots and kept running.

Carson ran parallel to the road towards where the confrontation with the girl was taking place. He halted for a moment and crouched in the cover of a large cactus.

On the edge of the road he could see the sleek bulk of the coach. Men were milling around looking back along the road towards the sound of the gunshots. For the moment all attention was focussed on the bandit Carson had felled. Henrietta Xavier and the uniformed man she had been struggling with were also looking up the road.

Carson came out of cover at a run. He took the little group by surprise. His target was the big man confronting the girl. He aimed the stock of the rifle he had taken from the guard at the man's head. In spite of his bulk the bandit chief moved surprisingly fast. The rifle hit his upraised arm as he blocked. Carson caught a glimpse of a blunt cruel face as the man snarled a curse at the youngster. Then he was ducking as the big man swung at him. The blow caught him on the side of the head and Carson staggered back almost going down with the force of the man's punch.

His opponent dropped his hand to his pistol. With one swift movement Carson slid his hammer from the sheath. He swung and the heavy hammer smashed into the man's arm. The blow was powerful enough to break the arm. There was a grunt and the man staggered sideways but did not go down. Instead he launched himself at Carson.

The attack forced the youngster to retreat. He tried to bring the hammer shaft to block the man's lunge but he was forced to give way. Abruptly he slammed into the side of the coach. The man used his uninjured arm to batter at Carson's head. The blows were unexpectedly forceful for a man with a broken wing.

The surprise gained by the swiftness of Carson's attack had caught the bandits off-guard. Becoming aware of the fight by the coach they were bringing their weapons to bear.

One of their number, obviously a second in command, began running towards the coach.

'Don't fire!' he screamed fearful of hitting the struggling bandit chief.

Carson could see his advantage slipping away. His attempt to rescue the girl was going badly wrong. The tenacity and strength of the man he attacked had taken him by surprise.

Seldom in his life had he met anyone who matched him in size and strength. Now he was being forced to give way before an ox of a man who should have been disabled by his initial attack. At this point he was rescued from an unexpected quarter.

Henrietta Xavier, who up till then had been ignored by the struggling men decided to take part in the action. Pulling a small revolver from her pocket, she fired point blank at Carson's attacker. The bright flash and report from the revolver was enough to distract the big man. He half turned towards this new danger.

Carson could not tell if the girl's shot had hit home. He aimed a vicious kick at the man's kneecap. Thrown off balance the man staggered away from the coach. This time the hammer crunched into the bandit chief's neck and he went down. By this time the bandit rushing to aid his chief was close. He raised his revolver and fired.

Carson heard the shot strike the coach. He brought his own weapon up — the first time he had an opportunity to fire it. The two rapid shots he triggered punched a dark hole in the bandit's chest. The man staggered the last few steps, his revolver dipping as his life bubbled out.

Carson's action acted as a spur to the rest of the rangers. Almost as one they launched an attack on their captors. Without arms some were mown down as they threw themselves forward. Others closed with the bandits and suddenly the road was filled with struggling shouting men. Carson lost no time. He reached out and gripped the girl by the shoulder. With rough strength he swung her towards the front of the coach.

'Mount up!' he yelled and quickly began to free the horses from the coach harness.

The girl was plucky. In spite of all that was happening around her she scrambled on to the horse. Pausing only to fire a couple of shots in the direction of the bandits heading towards the coach, Carson jumped on the second horse and thudded his heels into its flanks.

'Ride!' he yelled at the girl.

But she was already urging her mount forward. The girl went racing towards the broken-down wagon that had brought their little convoy to a halt.

Carson began firing his weapon at the few men he could see around the disabled wagon. Bandits scattered as they saw the muzzle flashes from his carbine. The two riders successfully skirted around the obstruction and headed down the open road.

They could hear firing from the men manning the road-block. Something burned the top of Carson's head, making him duck low over his mount. Another bullet creased his shoulder. Beside him he could see the girl urging her mount to faster speed. His vision became blurred as the wound on top of his head took effect. It did not help that he was bouncing along on top of a wildly galloping horse.

The road ahead was clear and they raced neck and neck towards freedom. As they fled along the road the crackle of rifle fire sounded behind them. But by now they were beyond range of accurate shooting and no more bullets came near.

Carson looked back. In the gloom he could just make out the shape of the broken-down wagon. Then they pounded round a bend in the road and he lost sight of the bandits.

He glanced at the girl. All he saw was the pale profile of a young girl as she urged her mount forward. Carson leaned across and shouted.

'The first chance we get we'll turn off the road. They'll be after us and we'll never outrun them.'

Ahead Carson saw a faint track leading away from the road.

'Down there,' he called. 'With a bit of luck they might miss where we turned off. But the further we get from this road the better.'

The girl guided her mount into the side road.

'Where are we going?' she asked.

'I'm not sure. If we're to avoid recapture then we'll have to travel as far as possible while it is still light,' he said. 'Our first priority is to put as many miles as possible between ourselves and those bandits.'

Even as he spoke darkness was descending.

'We'd better slow down a mite. It won't help if our horses go lame.'

The horses slowed to a canter. They rode like that as the darkness settled around them and for the time being neither was inclined to break the silence of the night.

4

The way station was just a group of single-story log buildings. Discarded harnesses and broken crates lay scattered around the buildings. They had stopped here from sheer necessity. Inside, the surly owner served them. The warm beer made a welcome change from the water they'd had to drink for the last few days.

They sat at a rough plank table and ate. Carson sipped his drink and spooned beans and sausages into his mouth. His stoical silence annoyed Henrietta. But he could not help that. He would speak when she spoke to him. The beautiful, sophisticated young woman overawed him. In the meanwhile he ate and contemplated the job he had to do.

With General Rodriguez raiding freely along the border, law and order had broken down and his men roamed unrestricted through the lawless lands. Up till now the young ranger had managed to evade the kidnappers he knew would be following them. He knew there was a long way to go before he could deliver the girl safely over to her father, Senor Xavier. The girl suddenly broke his train of thought.

'Do you have to be so sullen?'

Carson ceased chewing. He was at a loss to answer her question.

'I . . . I . . . beg your pardon, Miss . . . I . . . I don't know what you mean.'

To cover his confusion Carson took another mouthful of beans and pushed half a sausage into his mouth. It made an unsatisfactory and unappetising meal but it filled the stomach.

'And do you have to eat in that disgusting manner?'

Carson choked on the sausage and almost gagged as he tried to swallow it whole. He coughed suddenly and beans and partially chewed sausage spewed from his mouth. The look of disgust on the face of the girl was unsettling. He dropped the wooden spoon he had been using and covered his mouth with his hands. His face burned with embarrassment and his eyes were watering.

'Sorry,' he tried to apologise but this only resulted in more coughing.

The disdainful look the girl gave him had a more devastating impact on him than a back-swipe from her hand. In fact, given the choice he would have been happy to take a beating from her than have to endure the withering scorn she packed into that single look.

This was the aristocrat putting the peasant in his place. Generations of Spanish aristocracy were behind that scornful eye. Still coughing and sputtering he scrambled to his feet.

'Begging your pardon . . . ' he managed to stutter as he headed to the door.

'Wait!'

The command stopped him short.

'Where do we go from here?'

Still facing the door he answered, 'The station keeper has rooms. We can rest here. After a few hours sleep we start again. It should be well dark by then and safer for us to travel.'

He turned back to the door.

'I'm just going outside to see if the horses are all right.'

'Does it never occur to you to address me in the proper manner?'

Carson stood still. Sweat was breaking on him. In his short life he had never been in a more humiliating position. This girl with her haughty manners unnerved him as no other person ever had. In the two years with the Texas Rangers since the murder of his grandfather, even the tough men he served under had never managed to reduce him to this sweating nervousness.

To give himself time to think and recover somewhat he retrieved the great hammer from its resting-place on the floor and slung it over his shoulder. Only then did he look at the young woman staring arrogantly back at him.

She was tall and slender. Too skinny for his own taste, he had decided. Her face was pale and narrow with high cheekbones. She was more handsome than pretty. At the moment she looked washed-out and weary. However she was still able to stare at him with some distain.

'And how would you like me to address you — as your Royal Highness? Begging your pardon, ma'am, but I'm not used to the company of the upper classes.'

He could also have added he had met very few females in his short span of years. His job as smithy in Perdue had not brought him into contact with many women and his subsequent life in the rangers had also been lacking in female company. Now he was thrown unprepared into close contact with a sophisticated young woman and the fact that she was the daughter of the wealthiest man along the border was disconcerting.

'I . . . I . . . excuse me, I have to go now. I'll see to the horses. Then I have to clean my weapons and plan a route that will hopefully keep us out of danger and take us back to your father.'

Without giving her time to reply he strode to the door and stepped outside.

It was the faintest of movements — a tiny whisper of sound along with an uncanny instinct for survival that saved him from taking the rifle butt directly on the side of the head.

Instinctively he flinched and swung sideways. The rifle slammed into his shoulder and he crashed against the wall, almost going down. The sledge-hammer slid from his grip and bounced onto the dirt. The shaft of the hammer fell towards his attacker and this tiny accident was sufficient to distract the man from immediately following up his attack.

Even though his shoulder was numbed by the force of the strike Carson sent his whole body into overdrive. His good arm came up with the Bowie grasped in his hand. He drove the big blade into the belly of his huge attacker and angled it up inside the stomach. For a moment the man stood still while surprise and pain and shock washed across his swarthy countenance. Then the gutted man bellowed like a bull and clasped a hand to the wound opened in his belly. Strands of intestine began to bulge out from the vicious wound. The rifle dipped and fell from his other hand.

'You *bastardo*,' he managed to get out before the knife sliced once more into him.

This time Carson drove the blade into the man's throat. He did not wait to see the results of his savage attack but dropped on one knee while at the same time grabbing for his Colt. This instinctive action again saved his life.

A stream of bullets swept over his head and drove the already toppling body of the first attacker back inside the doorway.

Carson's own weapon fired and the two men aiming their rifles were smashed back to fall and lie twitching and bleeding in the dirt. His eyes scanned the corral but no more gunmen showed.

Nursing his numbed shoulder he stepped back over the body of the man who had attacked him.

Henrietta was standing by the table with hands straight out in front of her. Her pocket revolver was trained unwaveringly on Carson.

'Christ, it's me!' he hissed.

Slowly she lowered the gun. Her gaze dropped to the bright crimson wound in the dead man's neck. She made as if to say something but Carson ignored her. Swiftly he crossed the room.

Earlier he had looked around the back for an easy way of retreat if needed. Now he pushed open the back door and looked out. All he could see were mesquite bushes and cacti. Carson scanned these suspiciously. The foliage was an ideal cover for an ambush. Mysteriously the man behind the bar had disappeared.

The girl slid along the wall towards him, watching the doorway as if she expected to see another corpse come hurtling through.

He guided her out the back door and cautiously edged to the corner of the building until they came to the fence that bounded the coral. Their horses were still there along with several others. Beyond the corral he saw the trail leading south. There was no sign of life anywhere.

He sighed and relaxed somewhat.

'Let's see what supplies we can rustle up from this place,' he said and then pointed to the empty road. 'That's the road we have to take. Hopefully it will lead to your father and safety.'

5

Carson tiredly sat on his horse as it plodded along the muddy trail. He took stock of his resources. Besides his sledge, his pistol and rifle and his Bowie he had the saddlebags stuffed with what food they had found back at the way station. They had swapped their own tired mounts for the dead raiders' horses.

Left to his own devices Carson would have travelled light — living off the land. Now however he had the girl to consider and at all costs he must keep her safe.

His shoulder throbbed painfully and he was angry with himself for being caught so easily back at the way station. It never occurred to him that a part of the blame he might have attributed to the girl for behaving so churlishly towards him. He had stepped outside without his usual caution and had paid the price. It was a lesson learned and stored. He could not afford to slacken his vigilance.

Now they were following the route south but keeping a look out for riders. At first Carson had thought to travel across country but as the going was so rough and he was afraid of getting lost he had decided to keep to the road.

A faint lightening in the atmosphere warned him dawn was not far off. He would have to find a place to hide. On his own perhaps he would have carried on but he knew the girl would probably need rest and sleep before going any further. Then suddenly, in the gloom of the morning, he sighted the ranch house some distance ahead.

Carson loosened the carbine in its scabbard. He halted and Henrietta drew alongside.

'We'll try this place and see if they can put us up so we can shelter during the daylight hours.'

It was much easier going on the

cultivated land than riding along the rutted highway. Even so the horses stumbled, probably more from weariness than the uneven footing. He put out his arm to call a halt.

'Wait here while I go on and see what's up ahead.'

He left the horses with her. In spite of his strength and endurance he was glad to ease his legs after the long ride. Peering cautiously around him he slunk forward, keeping close to the rail fencing. In his hand he carried a long, keen-edged blade — the same blade that had sliced into his attacker back at the lodge.

There was no sound — no lights from the buildings. He guessed it was an isolated farm. At the gate he paused and then slid into the yard.

There was a metallic clink from his right and he jerked back bringing the knife round in an upswing. There was a scuffle of bare feet on cobbles — a snuffling and more clinking sounds and a low growling.

The eyes gleamed incandescent in the faint dawn light. The lips were drawn back from wicked teeth. With a low snarl the dog pounced. As he stepped back and brought up his knife the animal was brought up short on the end of its chain tethering it to the fence post. Carson edged past the dog, leaving it straining futilely after him.

Cautiously he moved towards the farmhouse. When he saw the broken front door he guessed the farm was deserted. Silently he stepped inside, peering into the dim interior.

It was a death house — that much he could smell.

The shotgun lay a few feet from the body of the dead rancher. He never had the chance to fire it. Flies rose in a swarm from the congealed blood. They settled again and crawled into the nostrils and the mouth lying open as if in a silent scream.

Edging past the sprawling body Carson explored the rooms. The place had been looted. There was no one else downstairs. Upstairs he found a mess of overturned furniture and ruptured drawers.

In the main bedroom he found the woman of the house or what had once been a woman.

She was spread-eagled on the bed her arms still bound to the posts with rawhide. Carson stared in fascinated horror. He had seen some gruesome things during his stint with the Texas Rangers but this savagery sickened him.

Here was an innocent man and woman eking out a living on their farm producing food in what must have been a life of unremitting toil. Now, in the bed where she had lain with her man she had been brutally raped and mutilated — her body used to relieve the perverse, sexual appetites of disturbed creatures that had never built nor grown anything useful in their lives.

The bedroom was sparsely furnished. An old dilapidated dresser stood by the window. The mirror was discoloured where the silvering had peeled. One or two worn rugs were scattered around on the bare floorboards.

In some ways the house reminded him of his own family home back in Perdue — the poor but honest family, doing their best to stay respectable in spite of the poverty. He shook his head trying to displace this morbid disquietude over the murdered couple.

When the faint noise in the landing reached him he jerked his hand back and pulled his gun only to stop and stare at the figure outlined in the doorway. The same horror he was feeling was reflected in the eyes of Henrietta as she stared at the ravaged woman on the bed.

Swiftly he moved to stand between the bed and the shocked gaze of the girl. Her stricken eyes searched his face as she moved through the doorway. Carson tried to block her but she pushed past him and stood staring in morbid befuddlement at the gross mutilation of the woman in the bed.

'The poor woman. Her husband is lying dead downstairs. What manner of brutes do things like this?'

The faint moan ghosted into the room like a draught from a graveyard. They stood in shocked silence. The sound when it came was almost too faint to be recognized.

For long, stretched out moments they stood there — like confined angels in this chamber of death. Almost as they became convinced they were mistaken, they heard it again.

Carson's breath went cold within his body. The hair on the back of his head began to prickle. He now knew where the sound was coming from but was unwilling to look or even admit to himself what it was. So fearful was he that his whispered denial was almost as faint as the original sound that so unnerved him.

He knew he had to make sure. There was sluggish caution in his movements as he turned to the tormented flesh on the bed. Hesitantly he moved forward and stood over the bloodied pulp that once had been a living, warm woman. This time there was no mistaking it. From that ravaged body issued another weak, almost inaudible groan and Carson moaned also.

His hand trembled visibly as he reached out. The woman's neck was bruised and bloody where savage teeth had left their brutal imprint. His fingers probed her neck searching for a pulse. It was almost with relief he believed she had succumbed. Then he found the pulse — insubstantial though it was — he knew in spite of her terrible ordeal the woman still lived. An awful feeling of helplessness and sorrow swept over him.

'Is she . . . she must be dead . . . '

'I . . . I'm not sure,' he lied.

Almost without conscious intent his knife appeared in his hand. He heard the gasp from Henrietta.

'What are you doing?'

His vacant eyes stared at her as if he

had been unaware of her presence. Her face was haggard with fatigue and distress. He looked down at the knife in his hand.

'What can I do?' he said helplessly.

6

Henrietta made a helpless movement with her hands. Bending over the breathing, bloody mess in the bed he thrust the knife against the rawhide that bound the woman to the bed. Henrietta helped Carson pull the crumpled blankets up to cover the ravaged woman. Then she stared at her companion, helplessness and anguish in her expression.

'A drink, perhaps there is something downstairs.'

They both started for the door.

'One of us ought to stay.'

Carson went downstairs. He dragged the body of the rancher outside, wincing a little at the pain in his injured shoulder.

The kitchen had been ransacked, as had the rest of the house. He found a bucket half-filled with water. Reluctantly he trudged upstairs with tin mugs.

While he supported the woman's head, the girl dribbled the liquid into her mouth. As she did this, the mutilated woman began a convulsive swallowing, making unnerving, sucking noises.

Carson broke into a sweat as he watched. He had intended to seek refuge in the dwelling — now they had no option. There was no way he could leave the woman even though he felt certain she could not survive. In an awful moment of truth he realized that the best thing was for the woman to succumb to her injuries. Death would be merciful.

'We'll have to stay here today. There's little chance of the bandits coming back again so soon. But we'll take no chances and watch for their return. We'll take it in turns to sleep. I think three-hour shifts should be sufficient. If that's all right with you?'

He had been talking in whispers as if afraid to waken the woman.

'One of us can watch and listen from

up here and the other find somewhere to bed down. We can't keep going on without sleep.'

'All right, shall I go first?'

He nodded. She headed for the door.

'It might be best to stay downstairs. There's a back door. It'll be easier to make a run for it if necessary.'

She nodded wearily, too drained by her ordeal to contribute much to the formulation of plans.

'There's a couch in the front room. Take some blankets with you.'

For a time he watched out of the window of the bedroom, acutely aware of the ravaged woman lying in the bed near him. At last he could stand it no longer and tiptoed downstairs and walked outside.

He made a circuit of the farmyard. It was only when he heard the clink of the chain that he remembered the dog. Slowly he approached the tethered animal. The dog bared its teeth and growled menacingly.

'Good dog,' Carson spoke gently. 'I

can't leave you here. You'll starve to death on the end of that chain. Are you going to behave while I free you?'

Leaving the dog straining after him Carson went back inside and rummaged in the kitchen. He found a barrel of salted meat that somehow had escaped the raiders. He selected a good-sized joint and walked back to the gate.

Slowly he edged forward, all the time talking softly. The dog stood trembling. It could smell the meat and the man was not menacing it in any way.

The dog had not been fed for two days. Now it was ravenous but torn between hunger and doing its duty. Hunger won and Carson watched as the dog tore greedily at the meat. While it chewed it watched Carson. He released the chain from the hook on the fence but retained the end in his hand.

'Come on, girl. Bring your supper with you.'

As he talked Carson turned back to the house still holding on to the lead.

The dog obediently picked up the joint of meat and trotted behind the man. He led it into the kitchen and dropped the chain to the floor.

As the dog flopped onto the earth floor and went back to worrying the meat Carson reached for the collar. For a moment the dog stiffened as the man groped for the clasp but it allowed him to remove the thick leather collar. It went back to the meat.

Carson watched as the dog ripped at the salted beef. His expression softened.

'I had a dog once. He was called Puma — about as tall as you but much bulkier. He came everywhere with me.'

The dog went on chewing; the only sign it heard the man was the twitching of the ears. With a sigh Carson rose from the chair and walked outside. He left the door open behind him. When the dog was ready it could escape.

He walked to the fence and leaned against it with his forearms resting on top. All was still around the ranch.

There was a slight sound behind him and he tensed. Then something gently pressed against him and he relaxed. The dog leaned against his leg and he could feel it trembling. He reached down and fondled its head. The dog eased its weight against him. Under his caresses the trembling abated then gradually ceased altogether.

Again Carson was reminded of his own big black Puma. And with that memory there came crowding into his mind the images of that former life as a smith in the peaceful village of Perdue. The painful memories of those early days welled up inside him. He tried to shut out the picture of his grandfather dangling on that rope on the fateful day that changed his life forever.

The dog heaved itself up and braced its paws against the rail beside him. He felt cold nostrils muzzling his ear. The dog sniffed along the side of his head. It was as if it was sensing his pain and was trying to comfort him.

He heard someone call his name and

he turned towards the voice. A bulky shape stood in the doorway of the farmhouse. It stood still and almost luminous in the light from the morning sky. The figure made no move towards him but stood there — an indeterminate silhouette. His heart hammered in his breast. He tried to call out but his throat would not work. He tried again.

'Grandad . . . ?'

The figure moved out into the yard.

His mouth was dry — his pulse pounding as he watched the essence move towards him. Suddenly he felt that everything was all right again. The violent past had been a dream. There had been no training as a ranger. He was just a simple smith hammering out a living in the steamy heat of the forge. Everything else had been a nightmare. The reality was with his granddad and his family.

'Gramps . . . ' he whispered the name again.

As he moved towards the figure his head jerked suddenly forward and he struck his forehead on the fence post against which he had been leaning. That painful slip woke him and he sagged against the wooden post. Shaken and disoriented by the dream, he stared in bewilderment about him.

The cold morning light remained still and empty. The ghosts had been imprisoned in his brain. Tiredness had released them. With a shuddering sigh he straightened and walked slowly back to the house. Behind him the fields that had sustained the rancher and his wife were becoming visible as the sun climbed into the morning sky.

7

Inside the farmhouse Henrietta stirred restlessly. She had fallen on to the sagging upholstery almost dizzy with exhaustion after watching by the bedside of the mutilated woman. Her thoughts were jumbled and troubled. From a life of privileged wealth she was reduced to hiding with a rough peasant in some miserable ranch miles from her home.

She longed to be with her father. Only he could give her the safety and protection she yearned for. In the meantime, the callow youth, Carson was to be her protector. In spite of all he had achieved she did not have much faith in his role as bodyguard. He was too young and inexperienced.

There was a soft noise outside the room. The bulky figure of a man loomed in the doorway.

'Miss Henrietta.'

Henrietta, half-asleep, put out a hand as if to ward off the intrusion. Panic filled her.

'It's me, Carson.'

'Yes, what is it?'

'I need to get some sleep. Would you keep watch for the last hours before it gets dark?'

'I suppose so.'

'There's a dog. It was the guard dog. It seems safe enough. I released it and fed it. I will have to introduce you so it will accept you.'

In spite of herself she had to stifle a giggle.

'Will it be a formal occasion?'

'When you are ready.'

He backed from the doorway. While she was rising from the makeshift bed she smiled wryly at the thought of being introduced to a dog. She found the man and dog waiting for her in the kitchen.

'It won't bite. I've kinda made friends with it.'

She took in the large, black dog

standing stiffly beside the man. His hand rested lightly on the animal's head.

'Walk slowly towards us.'

In spite of her dislike of being instructed by this oaf, nevertheless she did as he said.

'Good girl.'

For a brief and light-headed moment the girl wondered if he was addressing her or the dog. She reached out to the animal and felt its breath on her skin as it examined her. The dog sat back on its haunches and looked expectantly at Carson.

He smiled down at the animal and patted it on the head.

'When I released it I thought it would take off, but it seems to have attached itself to me. Perhaps when we move on it will remain here at the farm. Now I must sleep. Listen and watch from the windows. Any noise at all — horses, footsteps, voices — wake me immediately. Look in on the woman upstairs occasionally. There's been no change.'

He walked back into the room she had just vacated.

She disobeyed his instructions to stay indoors and walked outside into the bright afternoon. She was just in time to see the geese flying in their familiar vee-formation across the sky. The honking sound they made as they battered their way against the light wind was oddly reassuring. While the human herd was warring amongst themselves, nature carried on with the seasons and migrations.

She walked to the end of the yard and looked out across the countryside. The rancher had ploughed some of the fields and the slick dirt lay in neat folds like the ribs of some giant land monster. She wandered to the rear of the farmhouse but could see nothing beyond the barns and outhouses.

The muffled noise of a horse whinnying interrupted her thoughts. She stood rigid with tension waiting for the sound to repeat itself. Then it came again — the distinct neighing of a horse.

The first love in Henrietta's life was horses. The smell and sight of the great beasts had been some of her earliest memories. As a very young girl her mother had sat her up on the saddle in front of her and cantered around the estate. The small hands had gripped the coarse mane and cooed with delight.

As soon as she was able to sit up unaided she had ridden as often as she was permitted. Galloping across the countryside with the wind and occasional rain in her face was sheer heaven. The experience had given her a high she had never been able to equal in any other activity.

Nothing could match the sensations in her when, with her thighs wrapped round the powerful barrel of a steaming stallion, she thundered across the land — hair streaming out behind her and the feel of the surging muscles of the powerful beast she sat astride.

Slowly she walked towards the outbuildings. The thin light leaking from the horizon bathed the clapboard stable in weak sunlight. She walked to the rough wooden doors and gripped the handles.

The door opened easily on greased hinges and crunched against the stops. The familiar smells washed over her and she took a moment to breathe in the pungent animal odours. It was as welcome to her senses as the most expensive perfumes. She stepped inside and saw the blunt heads pushing over the stable doors eager for the sight of her.

'There, there,' she crooned and reached out to touch the familiar coarse forelocks.

There were a couple of stalls and both were occupied. The horses pressed forward butting their chests against the rope restraints and nickering with expectation. She looked for feed and water in their stall and could find none.

Still making soothing noises she found the hay and was soon busy stacking up their feed. It took a couple of trips with a bucket to replenish the

drinking troughs. She watched contentedly as the hungry and thirsty animals
ate and drank their fill.

So engrossed was she in these
pleasurable tasks that she failed to hear
the noise of horses heading up to the
ranch.

8

The pressure on his forehead was persistent. He moaned in his sleep and twisted away from the cold ring of metal boring into his head. But he was not yet fully aware of his actions or of the thing that was disturbing his sleep.

When he did come awake instinctive self-preservation kicked in. He rolled into the gunman taking the man's legs from under him and wrenched at the gun pressed into his temple. The man stumbled and fell to the floor but stubbornly held onto his weapon. Carson bit into the hand still clenched tight around the butt. With a muttered curse the man pulled the trigger.

The muzzle flash momentarily blinded Carson but he held grimly on to the pistol. Then something smashed into the side of his head. He crashed to the floor and rolled with the next blow, which missed his head but banged into his shoulder. It was the same shoulder that had been injured last night.

The pain from the blow lanced across his shoulder and pulsed into his arm. The limb went numb as Carson struggled to his feet. A boot hit him in the face and he crashed over on to his back. At the same time a shot rang out splintering the door behind him. Carson hesitated, unable to see where the shot had come from.

'You just stay where you are, amigo. The next move and you'll get a bullet in the head.'

Helplessly lying on his back he squinted up at the figures surrounding him. Armed bandits stood around the room. They held weapons and all were trained on him.

Carson lay there waiting developments. Any sudden movement on his part and he knew the guns would blast him to shreds. His next thought was for the girl.

What a fool he had been — leaving

her on guard! But he'd had no option. When he had lain down he had intended to rest only briefly. But the stress and lack of sleep had taken their toll and he had dropped into a deep slumber only to be brutally awakened by these men. There was a noise from outside and he could feel the tension heighten in the men guarding him. A sudden scream and the noise of a scuffle came from outside the room.

'It's a girl, Romero. I've got her.'

A man's voice cursed out loud.

'Oh, ya coyote bitch!'

The unseen struggle continued. Carson tensed for an opportunity to take advantage of any easing of vigilance from his captors.

'Don't even think about it, amigo,' a voice grated out.

This time he saw the man who spoke. As he stared up at him Henrietta was pushed into the room, looking dishevelled and angry. She was struggling against the clutches of the two men shoving her in to the room.

'Well, well, what have we here — a sleeping giant and a . . . '

In mid sentence the voice broke off abruptly. The girl glared angrily at the speaker. He in turn gave a low whistle.

'If I'm not mistaken we have awoken a sleeping giant and found a missing princess.'

A moment's silence followed this observation.

Carson watched the men standing around the room. They were heavily armed with rifles and bandoleers of ammunition. Carson cursed inwardly. These were very like the men who had ambushed the coach. Their leader was a lean, hawk-faced man. Several days beard growth adorned his lean cheeks. He bowed from the waist.

'Pardon Senorita, it seems we have come in the nick of time to rescue you.'

'Romero, what are you trying to tell us?' One of the armed men asked.

'Bend your knees, you common dogs. You are in the presence of aristocracy. Next to our beloved leader this is the nearest thing to a person of privileged wealth you will ever get to see.'

The man walked over to the girl and hooked his hand beneath her chin. The girl stared defiantly up at him.

'Don't forget, I worked for Senor Xavier before joining up with General Rodriguez. His daughter would not remember me, a mere groom in the stables, but I remember her. It was rumoured that you were missing, Senorita. How fortunate you fell in with me. I'm sure General Rodriguez will welcome you with open arms.'

Carson's fist crashed into the scrotum of the man holding the gun at his head. The gun went off and though the bullet missed him the muzzle flash burned the side of his face. A boot thudded into his side and instinctively he grabbed for it. He wrenched at the limb and the man fell across his body as a burst of gunfire thundered out. The body jerked as bullets hammered home. Carson was desperately feeling over the corpse searching for a weapon.

'Cease fire! Cease fire!'

Carson's hand closed on a weapon. He jerked to free it from the corpse lying across him. Somehow it snagged and he couldn't clear it from the clothing of the dead bandit.

'The girl dies if you don't give up, Senor!'

Carson looked across the room. Romero had a pistol in his hand. It was pressed against the head of Henrietta. She was standing perfectly still. Carson took in the rest of the room.

A ring of rifles like the dark eyes of venomous serpents stared down at him. He did not think the bandit would shoot the girl but he knew the odds of him surviving the fire from so many weapons at such close range were stacked against him. Slowly he relaxed and let go of the revolver he had been trying to retrieve. Letting his hands fall to the floor he spread them wide.

'It's OK. I give up.'

Still holding the gun to Henrietta,

Romero issued curt orders. Carson was brutally kicked over onto his face. Cords were wrapped around his wrists so tight he winced as he felt the rawhide bite into flesh.

'Where did you find her anyway?' Romero quizzed the men who had dragged the girl indoors.

'She was in the stables. There're a couple of horses in there.'

'*Bueno*, we'll take the horses. Then we'll take these two with us to General Rodriguez.'

He turned back to the captives.

'It was lucky we found you. The country is swarming with bandits.'

He smiled at his own feeble joke.

'I smell a big reward in this for me. Don't either of you spoil it for me by trying to escape. It wouldn't go down well with General Rodriguez if I had to shoot his hostage. I imagine it would rather ruin your bargaining value.'

The captain bowed low towards the girl.

'Your noble escorts await, Senorita.'

The girl cast one forlorn glance at Carson before she was ushered out into the yard. No such courtesy was reserved for Carson. A rifle butt smashed into the middle of his back. Under a hail of blows he stumbled out into the yard.

Henrietta was handed up on horseback while a rope was knotted around Carson's neck and the other end tied to a saddle.

For one awful moment Carson saw the body of his granddad swinging on the end of a similar rope. Black rage swelled within him.

These were Rodriguez's men — the men against whom he had sworn vengeance. His arms tensed as he tested the strength of his bonds. Then he saw the ominous shape of the dog lying in the yard.

Slowly the rage subsided. The dog reminded him of his own mortality. Any one of these men would shoot him down.

Unarmed and trussed he stood very little chance of breaking free and killing the entire group. He might kill a few of the bandits but there were too many of them. For the moment the odds were stacked against him. He would bide his time. Somewhere in the course of events someone would make a mistake. When that moment came he would be ready. His revenge would come but it would not be today. The riders moved forward and the rope jerked tight around his neck.

'There's a wounded woman in the upstairs bedroom . . .'

No one heard his plea. His words were lost as the patrol moved out. He tried to shout again but his voice was a croak lost in the general noise of men pushing eagerly forward to get back to their camp.

Bleeding from his cuts and aching from the bruises on his body, Carson had to break into a trot in order to keep from being pulled off his feet. With his hands tied behind his back and a rope around his neck this was going to be a very uncomfortable journey.

9

General Rodriguez was the son of the Duke of Castille and had been sent to the Texas border to command the troops stationed there as a deterrent to Texan aggression. The title of general he had bestowed upon himself — and the uniform that went with it.

Overtly loyal to the Mexican government, covertly Rodriguez had, over the months of campaigning, replaced the men in his forces who were loyal to the government of Mexico with men he trusted to do his own bidding. The purging of men loyal to the central government had of necessity been a brutal and murderous campaign for Rodriguez and his closest lieutenants. It had been a long and bloody path to supreme robber chief along the borderlands.

Opponents and indeed sometimes

allies had been ruthlessly disposed off. Nothing was allowed to stand in his way. His ambitious mind was casting further afield now that he had consolidated his position along the borders of northern Mexico.

While pledging loyalty to the government he had been recruiting deserters and mercenaries. Gaining in strength and confidence he began to covet a position of power in Mexico itself.

In order to achieve that, he needed power and money. The attempt to abduct Henrietta Xavier had been planned with the objective of obtaining money from her father for her safe return. Rodriguez had also hoped to force Don Xavier to back him in his bid for power.

The Place of Holy Bones was a ruined monastery set beneath the grandeur of high sweeping hills and was rumoured to be a medieval settlement, with a history intimately entwined with the Roman Catholic order of Franciscans.

Early in the century the Apaches

massacred the entire congregation. The murder is assumed to have been an attempt to take over the magic the monks were supposed to use. It became a place of ghosts and superstition. For General Rodriguez it was just one of the many stopovers he used for his unlawful operations.

It was here Romero took his captives. The girl was kept under close watch in the old semi-ruined monastery. Carson was tethered to the large stone crucifix in the crumbling adobe chapel.

For Carson it had been a question of survival. Stoically he endured the journey back to the headquarters of General Rodriguez and his imprisonment in the old church.

The men guarding him had been told he was dangerous but as companion to Senorita Henrietta was to be treated well but kept tied up. He endured the hours of boredom by picturing the vengeance he would exact on General Rodriguez when the opportunity presented itself.

He observed and listened carefully to every scrap of information regarding Rodriguez's intentions and was especially interested in any information regarding Henrietta.

While he waited he was compliant and obedient, feeling that his very passivity would lull his guards into a feeling of security. When the time was ripe he would make his move. Now was not the time. So he watched and waited knowing that at some point he would seize a favourable opportunity to make a break for freedom.

The first meal of the day never varied — a bowl of cornmeal, a handful of leathery tortillas and a mug of luke-warm coffee. Under the guns of his guards Carson ate and drank everything placed in front of him for he knew he needed to keep up his great strength.

Everything he did and learned while in captivity was geared to the objectives of escape and vengeance. Then one day the monotony of captivity was broken when he was allowed a visitor.

A guard stepped inside the dim-lit chapel holding a flickering torch and a pistol. Blinking his eyes against the unaccustomed light the prisoner looked up.

'We got a visitor for you, big man.'

Carson watched as the woman picked her way through the rubble that littered the floor of the old crumbling church. For a moment he did not recognize her. She was dressed in some sort of expensive flowing gown. Over this was a caped jacket fastened at her throat with a gold clasp. The sleeves of the jacket seemed overly long and covered the woman's hands.

Carson stared stoically at the sudden vision of bright femininity in that dismal place. Taking everyone by surprise the girl rushed forward and flung her arms around Carson. No one was more surprised than Carson himself for it was only as she was close that he recognized Henrietta.

During their time together the girl had showed not the slightest sign of affection towards him. Now she was hanging around his neck and saying things that made no sense.

'Oh you poor man. Are they treating you all right? Why are you tied up like this?'

Then her voice went low and she whispered instructions to him.

'Bide your time. I will find some way to come to you.'

From the entrance of the chapel came a sharp laugh. Carson looked at the man as he stepped inside. At once he recognized the big man he had fought when rescuing Henrietta. The man's arm was in a sling and a bandage had been tied around his head where he guessed Henrietta's shot had wounded him.

He knew then he was looking at his sworn enemy and the image of an old man swinging on the end of a rope suddenly obscured his vision. Black fury swelled up with dizzying speed. His body tensed — great muscles swelling in anticipation of killing rage. Then a surprising thing happened. The girl stepped back from him and slapped him hard across the face.

He stared down at this girl who dared to strike him. She gazed passionately back at him.

'That's for being so off-hand with me. I thought I deserved more respect from you.'

Slowly he raised his bound hands and touched his cheek where she had struck him. Looking at her, his rage slowly diminished as he rubbed his face. She had sufficiently distracted him from committing a foolish act of bravado.

'Now you must be a good boy and behave. I just might allow you to resume your old duties as my personal servant.'

This time there was real amusement in General Rodriguez's laugh as he moved up the chapel and stood looking at the prisoner. The man Carson had sworn to kill was almost within reach. Carson kept his eyes on the girl. His rage had subsided, leaving him as suddenly as it had appeared.

Now was not the time. He could wait. Slowly he relaxed his muscles as he puzzled over the words of the girl. She had intimated he was to resume his duties as servant but he had never been her servant. He felt there was information in her words. For the moment he felt the odds were beginning to tip in his favour. With the girl loose and as anxious as him to escape maybe there was a way to get at his hated enemy.

Carson raised his head and stared sullenly at the man he held responsible for the murder of his grandfather.

The bandit chief was a big man. His skin was swarthy and he had dark, wiry, close-cropped hair. A carefully shaped beard adorned his chin and lips. His face was round and slightly chubby. From the lobe of his left ear a large gold ring dangled. The man looked appreciatively at Carson. Slowly he walked around the prisoner.

'Why is he tied up like an animal?' Henrietta asked.

'Dangerous animals are kept caged

and chained. This man looks as if he could take on a legion of my guards and eat them for breakfast. I'm glad you brought me down here. Seeing him has given me an idea.'

Rodriguez stopped beside Henrietta and stood looking at Carson.

'How would you like to be free, amigo? Perhaps to continue your duties as Henrietta's servant?'

Carson said nothing, waiting for him to continue. He knew the man was not offering a free passage. The bandit was not that sort of man.

'In a few days, it is the festival of St Lohair and we will be staging a tournament. The champion, Gondor the Great is expected to win. How would you like to go against this champion and win your freedom by defeating him?'

Carson stared sullenly back at his enemy. In his mind he was not fighting Gondor the Great but was slowly and deliberately strangling the man before him.

10

The atmosphere of anticipation in the ancient Place of Holy Bones in the lead up to the festivities was almost palpable. The event most talked about was the proposed duel of the champions. The duelists must fight with hand-weapons only — clubs, knives, swords, axes, spears were all acceptable. No firearms were allowed.

The grand finale to the festival was slowly being acted out on the turf of what had once been a bullring. This event was the aptly named Bouts of the Brutal. Two full days were devoted to this event. The crowd loved it. Men fought to the death in the arena. In some fights the protagonists were unable to continue because of serious injury. One man stood head and shoulders above all other contestants.

Gondor the Great had maimed and

killed his way into infamy in the arena. He was the acknowledged champion. Now he served the bandit chief as a member of his bodyguard.

As the champion, Gondor did not take part in these bouts. However he was there at each match as an observer while the combatants duelled. His main objective was to note the strengths and weaknesses of the duellists he may have to meet at sometime in the future, for at the end of the games the overall winner was given the opportunity to challenge the champion. Very often the victor declined the invitation to go up against the notorious killer.

Already the crowd was wild with excitement. They had watched two young warriors knife each other into bloody incapacity. The young men had been carried from the arena with honour intact.

Another bout ended in a similar stalemate as two men fought with lances. Their weapons rang and clashed as they duelled backwards and forwards across the arena. The crowds yelled encouragement. For some moments the lancers seemed evenly matched. Then one took a cut across the shoulder and back-peddled furiously. His opponent, sensing his advantage, swung his weapon mercilessly trying to inflict a killing wound. He was too eager and took a slash across the chest that opened a long gash.

Both men, blood pouring from their wounds, fought on more warily, each searching for an opening. Then the man who had taken the first wound received a thrust to the chest severe enough to put him down. As he fell he jabbed his weapon forward and pierced his opponent in the groin.

Both men were on the ground bleeding profusely, hands clasped over slashed flesh, unable to continue. Seeing the bout could not be concluded the match was called to a halt. The wounded men were carried from the ring. So the eliminating fights would continue till after two bloody days, one man was at last declared the overall winner.

'Will you fight Gondor?'

For a moment only, Carson held Rodriguez's gaze. He nodded. The bandit chief smiled and turned to signal his champion. The big man ambled over. His bulk was awesome.

Carson gazed across at the hulk who in turn was eyeing him up. He would fight, for it would make him closer to Rodriguez and when he was close enough he would kill the man responsible for the slaying of his grandfather.

There was of course the girl to be considered. Carson, with his sense of honour, still felt responsible for her. He smiled grimly to himself.

Here he was with his hands and feet tied with rawhide thongs and about to go up against their undefeated champion and he was making plans to kill a man surrounded night and day by bodyguards.

On top of that he was worrying about his duties as the protector of Henrietta.

Now was not the time for such thoughts. Right now he had a duel to fight and by the look of his opponent it was not going to be an easy affair.

At a nod from Rodriguez, Carson was released from his bonds. Slowly he massaged the rawhide indents from his wrists as he sized up his opponent.

Gondor was a big man — bigger even than Carson. However the youngster noted the champion was running to fat. There were the telltale puffy layers around the eyes and the indication of a paunch. Too much soft living and no real opposition in recent bouts had begun to take their toll upon the champion. The two men eyed each other up.

'Gringo bleed like pig,' Gondor taunted.

Carson ignored the insult. He was looking around for the weapons they were to fight with. A bandit stepped up and held his hand for attention.

'Gondor will fight the Americano, Carson.'

The roar from the onlookers was filled with anticipation. Gondor was their all time favourite. They roared and stamped their feet and waved weapons in the air. They jeered and called insults down on the gringo dog. Carson watched all this impassively. He still couldn't see any weapons for the combatants.

'They will fight with bare fists,' intoned the bandit, acting as compere.

The noise from the bandits was continuous. It was an animal scenting blood. This was a fitting climax to the games. Their champion would batter the American to death. Their blood lust would be sated. Tonight they would sit around the campfires and boast about their champion.

Carson looked down at his hands. He balled them into fists and looked critically at them. A bare-knuckle contest!

He had seen such fights back in his native Perdue. Men stood toe to toe and slugged it out till one went down and couldn't get up again. They were bloody affairs. It would take strength and endurance to survive such a contest. He had never fought with his fists before, always preferring to use a weapon.

His opponent was strutting around grinning widely. He was shaking his huge meaty fists triumphantly at the crowd. They loved him for it. This was his event. This is what he had built his reputation upon. The men he fought never fought again. Once he had his man on the floor he would stomp him to death.

Impassively Carson watched his opponent — noted how he moved, how he planted his feet, the size of his arms as he gestured to the crowd. He flexed his own arms and shoulders and bent his knees a few times to loosen up.

The referee was calling the two men to the centre of the arena. They stood opposite and each weighed up his opponent. Gondor stabbed a blunt forefinger at Carson.

'You die, gringo pig.'

The big Mexican had shed his jacket and shirt and was clad only in breeches. Everything about him was huge. His arms and shoulders were bulky with muscle while his legs were like the proverbial tree trunks. Carson was clad in buckskins that covered a body honed and strong.

'May the best man win, Carson.'

Carson reached out to shake hands. As they gripped Gondor tightened his hold and pulling the young ranger towards him swung a sledgehammer blow with his huge meaty left fist.

Carson had fought many practice bouts with Bowie knives. He had slashed and cut and probed seeking weaknesses in his opponent's defences. During these practice matches with fellow rangers while engaged in trying to score points his opponent likewise was busily trying to score against him.

In the early days his reactions were not always so fast as to avoid penalties. The sparring taught a man to think and react swiftly. With this experience behind him Carson was able to duck beneath the swing and give a quick jab into the other man's ribs with his free hand. It was not a hard blow for he was off-balance but it caused the big Mexican to disengage and back away.

The blood contest had begun.

11

The two men circled warily, feinting and sizing each other up. They sparred for a short time and then the Mexican rushed in and smashed two blows into Carson's body. The youngster went back desperately trying not to go down for he had seen men knocked down in a fight and then a boot had cracked open a skull or crushed a windpipe.

His opponent kept after him, hustling him and making him go backwards. As he dodged past the pummelling fists a foot lashed out and took him in the thigh. Caught off-balance, Carson went down.

The crowd was wild with excitement. This was the beginning of the end. Their champion was on form.

Desperately Carson rolled trying to avoid the stomping feet. Sudden searing pain erupted on the side of his head as his opponent's boot grazed his ear. He feared his ear had been torn off.

With an agility that seemed impossible in such a big man he catapulted to his feet and backed away rapidly. His breath came in heavy gulps. That was close. He could not afford to go down again.

A large meaty fist thudded into the side of his head and he stumbled back, desperately trying to keep on his feet. There would be no second chance if he went down again. Gondor would stomp his head into the earth.

Now they slammed blow for blow, each man confident in his own strength but as the bout went on and as blood flowed from both men they became more wary. The contest settled down to a sparring match as they probed for an opening, needing that crippling blow that would down the other.

Carson used his fists like he would have used the hammers from his old forge. Indeed, years of pounding the hot metal and toiling at the heavy work had hardened and strengthened his hands to the consistency of the metal with which he had worked. Now the clenched fists hammered mercilessly at the big fighter, slowly turning that brutal face to the consistency of raw beef.

Carson suspected he looked as bad as his opponent did. Gondor could only see properly out of one eye, for Carson's steady pounding had beaten his face into a swollen pulp. Blood oozed from the fighter's ears and nose and bloody spittle dribbled from bruised and distended lips. The big man was forced to breathe through his mouth for his nose was crushed.

A punch had opened a gash above Carson's right eye and he had to keep flicking blood from that eye in order to clear his sight. His ribs hurt from a close encounter in the bear-like grip of the giant Mexican. He had only escaped serious injury by head-butting Gondor on his already bruised and bleeding nose. His opponent had not been able to stand the fresh agony and had released Carson, desperately moving back out of range of his punches.

Neither man heard the jeers of the crowd. They had long ceased to take notice of anything outside their own little world of survival.

The bandits were roaring for a result. They had seen enough blood spilled — now they wanted a kill.

They screamed for Gondor to kill the Americano. They wanted a sacrifice — a blood sacrifice.

Bloodthirsty crowds like this had existed since the dawn of time. They watched dog fights, badger fights, bull fights, cock fights. If any creature could be matched against another in fighting then it was done.

The bandits roared and shouted and moaned out their blood lust and waited impatiently for the kill. However, when the end came it was a messy and unsatisfactory affair.

Carson was weary. He staggered with exhaustion. His opponent looked in a sorry condition also but he kept on punching, feinting, and blocking. Carson was retreating slowly looking for an opening.

This was not his sport at all. He had thought that his strength and youth and fitness would easily win this fight. Now he was not so sure. The Mexican had proved a skilled pugilist and now the scales were balanced evenly.

Carson was being forced back by the oncoming Gondor. The fighter was a bruising bear snorting his rage against the upstart youngster who had come against him. Nothing could stop him. He swung wildly at Carson — and missed.

In the ordinary course of events Gondor would have recovered and followed with another punch. This time he overbalanced and in his weariness he went down on one knee. Carson saw his chance and launched himself forward. With a two handed swipe he smashed a blow into the side of Gondor's jaw so that the bear keeled over, momentarily stunned. Again Carson lunged forward.

The edge of his stiffened hand struck Gondor in the throat, the blow crushing his larynx. Choking, the big man hung desperately to the edges of consciousness. His mouth was wide open, gasping for breath. He thrashed about on the dusty earth in agonized struggles. Carson moved in for the coup de grace.

Again he chopped with the side of his hand against the neck of the man. The big man tried to wriggle away from his attacker. Carson brought up his bloodied fist then paused. He was hesitant to kill his helpless opponent. Then for a brief moment he saw another big man swinging on the end of a rope. He drove his fist into the Mexican's gullet.

Gondor arched his back, his mouth open in a silent scream as he struggled for air. His hands grasped at his ruined throat. The eyes bulged as his brain was starved of air. Carson stepped back and lowered the fist poised to deal another blow. Somehow he knew it was unnecessary.

Impassively he watched his opponent roll about in agony. The big man thrashed around gagging and fighting for breath, his struggles growing weaker and weaker.

Carson turned and walked away. It took all his willpower to stay upright.

The crowd of bandits erupted — screaming spite and abuse at him like an enraged and frustrated beast. This upstart gringo had defeated their hero and they hated him for it.

The sound washed around Carson as he stood there swaying on his feet, his head drooping. Then he was being escorted from the arena and standing before the bandit chief. The man he hated smiled indulgently at him.

'Well, it looks as if you have won your freedom. You may take up your old position as Senorita Henrietta's servant.'

General Rodriguez turned and smiled at the girl. She sat there staring impassively over the top of Carson's head. Rodriguez turned his attention back to the bruised and bloodied champion.

'Amazing. I never thought I'd see Gondor defeated.'

Carson said nothing. He just wanted to crawl away and lie down somewhere quiet and begin the healing process. As if reading his mind, Rodriguez called out to his men.

'Take him away but take good care of him. He is our new champion.'

Carson was dismissed. As he was led away he stumbled and the men escorting him moved in and supported him. He did not protest. Weariness swept over him and he just wanted a place to lie and the chance to sleep. Thoughts of revenge were on hold for now. The more immediate needs of his body clamoured for his attention. Right now he needed rest and time to recover from his brutal ordeal in the arena.

12

The hand was across his mouth and the sharp blade pricked his throat. It was a soft delicate hand. A tantalizing perfume tickled his nostrils. He lay very still.

The inside of the room was in darkness. He could make out nothing. For a few moments he lay motionless — allowing the hand to press down on his lips. He wondered if he should snatch the knife and disarm the intruder, but instead he lay there patiently awaiting developments. If the person wanted him dead they could easily have done it while he slept.

'Carson,' the voice whispered, 'don't cry out — don't make a sound.'

Against the restraining hand he attempted to shake his head and mumbled into the palm. He recognized the voice and his guess was confirmed.

'It's me, Henrietta.'

The pressure of the blade on his throat eased. He was sure he could feel the wetness of blood where the girl had pressed too eagerly with her knife — not that a pinprick from Henrietta would cause him much distress in view of the damage inflicted on him during his fight with Gondor.

'What is it? Why are you here?'

'There's been a night of feasting. Everyone's making merry. I think we could make a break for freedom. Most of the guards are asleep or drunk.'

Slowly Carson sat up. It was not caution or fear of making a noise that made him so tardy. His body was a sea of pain from the pounding he had received at the fists of the big Mexican.

During his stint with the rangers he had been forced to punish his body with gruelling rides and with the possibility of vicious gunfights at the end. He knew what suffering his body could take and how long it would take to make a recovery. Right now he needed about a week of complete rest and masses of nourishing food. That would have to wait.

During his captivity the hatred he felt for Rodriguez had worked like a spur to help him survive. Now it seemed the chance to take his revenge for the murder of his grandfather was about to present itself.

'Where is Rodriguez now?' he asked.

His body was one raw mass of pain as he eased himself to his feet.

'He's in one of the cabins with his women. I fed whiskey to my guards. They're as drunk as priests now. It is a golden opportunity for us to escape.'

Carson nodded and then wished he hadn't. It was as if someone had peeled back the top of his scalp and poured burning kerosene into his head. The pain threatened to paralyse his neck and head.

'I . . . I watched you fight.' The girl's voice was hesitant. 'Somehow I knew you would come through . . . '

Her voice faltered and he suddenly

wondered if she was trying, in her own awkward way, to pay him a compliment. He dismissed the thought then stood up.

The room went spinning around and he felt himself tilt off-balance. The girl reached out to restrain him. She might as well have tried to check a falling tree. He spun away and almost went down as waves of dizziness and nausea wracked his body. Somehow he managed to keep upright. Vaguely he was aware of the girl pushing the neck of a bottle into his mouth.

'Swallow.'

His throat convulsed as he gulped down the raw spirits. He swayed unsteadily trying to stay erect. His eyes were out of focus as he tried to look at the girl.

'What . . . what was that?' he managed to croak.

There was a burning sensation in his guts. The girl swam in front of him as if there were a fall of water between them. He wanted to reach out and touch her

— to see if she were real. His arm floated up and he stared at it unsure if it were his own. Somehow the pain had dimmed. Gradually his vision cleared and in the murky gloom of the hut he saw the face of Henrietta peering anxiously up at him.

'Senorita Henrietta, I am your loyal protector . . . ' he mumbled.

'Yes, yes,' she replied impatiently, 'we have to find our way out of here now.'

Every moment he could feel himself stronger as the raw alcohol surged through his blood. Though fuzzyheaded his thoughts began to come together.

'There is something needs to be done before we go,' he said. 'I have to find General Rodriguez. You'll have to show me where he is.'

'What on earth are you on about? Rodriguez is holding us prisoner. He'll never let us go if he finds us wandering around loose.'

'You don't understand. I have a promise to keep.'

The fuzziness was still there and the

pain but as the alcohol coursed through his body he was beginning to function to a certain degree.

'Rodriguez is my enemy. I have to find him and kill him. I made a promise I would kill the man who murdered a member of my family. Now I am this near to him I can't let the opportunity pass for revenge.'

'You stupid man! We may only get one chance to escape and this is it. Yes, I know Rodriguez must die but you and I on our own in the middle of a bandit camp won't accomplish it.'

He stared stubbornly at her.

'You don't understand. I have to do this thing.'

She glared at him then spoke in a cool controlled voice.

'Did you or did you not take an oath of allegiance to the rangers?'

He blinked at her a few times, puzzled by her change of tack.

'Yes, I did. When I became a ranger I had to swear allegiance.'

'Do you know who I am?'

'Of course, you're Senorita Henrietta Xavier.'

He could feel himself stronger and more confident now.

'And whose daughter am I?'

Her voice was honey dripping from a spoon. Even through the alcohol daze he could see what was coming. He turned aside.

'I have a man to kill,' he said stubbornly.

'I asked you a question.'

The honey had disappeared. The queen bee was rousing herself — asserting her authority.

'Dammit! I know who you are! Haven't I been safeguarding you for the past week or so?'

'Exactly. And where does your sworn allegiance place you now?'

He sighed and rubbed his face with both hands.

'Rodriguez's thugs hanged my grandfather — an old man. He was a father to me. I . . . I . . . they hanged him like a dog . . . in the street. I cut him down.

I swore I would kill Rodriguez. I can't go back on my word.'

She was silent then as she thought this over. When she finally spoke her voice was low and firm.

'I can understand your bitterness and probably I would feel the same in your place. But now is not the time or the place. Look at you. You can barely stand. The only thing keeping you on your feet is the tequila I gave you. When that wears off you'll be aching and tired again. There are dozens of Rodriguez's men in this place. I know some are drunk but if the alarm goes up there will be enough of them to round you up and kill you. You won't get anywhere near Rodriguez.

'Your duty right now is to me and to the rangers. Rodriguez means to launch an attack into Mexico and take over as a dictator. He needs the backing of my father and intends using me to force him to do his bidding. I have to get away from here. If you fling your life away in a vain attempt to kill Rodriguez then he may never be defeated. My father needs us. He needs the information I can bring him. Now if you have any sense of loyalty then that loyalty must be to the rangers' code of honour.'

He took his hands from his face. His eyes were bloodshot and wild.

'Perhaps you're right,' he said at last. 'Maybe we can steal some mounts.'

The die was cast. He would give up his chance for revenge to get the girl out of this place and back to her father.

Her words had stung him. She had been under his protection and he had let her down. Now there was a chance for redemption. He would deliver the girl safely to her father and then come back for Rodriguez.

'Let's go.'

13

'If we walk along with confidence and purpose, then no one should bother us. We must make it seem as if I was on some errand and you are my escort.'

There were two guards watching over the remuda. Large men, made surly by the knowledge that while they were on sentry duty their companions were carousing.

They eyed the girl and her battered escort with suspicion. Carson could think of nothing to explain why he and Henrietta were interested in the horses. He was wondering which of the men to attack first when the girl spoke.

'General Rodriguez — I'm supposed to meet him here. He promised to show me his favourite mare. He knows how fond I am of horses.' Henrietta paused and frowned suddenly. 'He hasn't gone ahead of us already?'

The guards stared at her with hostility then looked uncertainly at each other.

Carson watched the two men, instinctively knowing they were going to argue. Swiftly he stepped forward and drove his fist into the kidney of the one nearest him. The man grunted and bent double. Carson's knee caught him in the face and he went down and stayed down.

Carson almost keeled over himself as his injured hand smashed into the guard. He stepped back with a sharp intake of breath, abruptly reminded of his injuries. His hands had been badly bruised during his bout with Gondor. The urgency of the present situation had made him forget the damage to his own body.

Nursing his hand he turned his attention to the second guard. The man was staring at Carson with sheer hatred in his face. He raised his rifle but before he could line it up he staggered back and crashed into the ropes corralling the ponies. The shaft of a knife protruded from his chest. He turned his head and with bloodshot eyes stared balefully at Carson. The young ranger watched in relief as slowly his opponent slid to the floor and lost interest in everything. He looked with renewed respect at Henrietta.

'Why didn't you tell me you had a knife. It might have saved me hurting my hands.'

He stepped forward and retrieved the knife and wiped it on the dead guard's clothes before returning it to the girl.

'Come on,' she said as she took the knife from him. 'We should be able to get a couple of ponies now.'

They were turning to the corral when a figure loomed up out of the darkness. A low call momentarily stopped them.

'*Amigo*, Senor Carson, where you go?'

Carson turned and saw a young Mexican grinning at him.

'Diego, fearless fighter at your service — willing to help you escape from

General Rodriguez.'

He grinned at the couple staring at him in the gloom.

'I come in friendship. Let me join you and I'll be your slave evermore.'

Henrietta turned and ducked into the corral. Carson hesitated torn between the man's request and the retreating back of the girl.

'Come,' she called imperiously in a voice that was not used to being disobeyed. 'We have no time for this!'

But Carson nodded to the young bandit.

'If it ain't a trick you can come along,' he said.

'Oh, for God's sake,' Henrietta exclaimed. 'How to make a successful escape! Take every stray dog that comes along.'

Diego stooped over the fallen guards and searched them. His quest was successful and he stood up with two pistols. He grinned as he handed one of them to Carson who had already purloined one of the carbines.

'God is bountiful.'

Carson was beginning to take to the brash young bandit. Diego then turned his attention to Henrietta. He bowed low before her.

'Beauty and the beast. Your highness, I beg your indulgence. Please allow me to accompany you and this awesome warrior who felled the mighty Gondor. There will be songs sung about your champion. They will be singing around the campfires in years to come. This mighty warrior is formed from the heroes of ancient lore.'

Carson groaned out loud. Diego looked at him with some concern.

'You are still weak from your battle, amigo?'

'It's not so much that as having to listen to this goddarned rubbish from you. If you fight as well with your fists as you do with your tongue then we shall have no trouble escaping from this place.'

Diego grinned widely.

'It is good to be with such a

comrade-in-arms.'

Carson moved to the side of the girl.

'We must hurry, before any alarm is raised.'

She gave him a withering glance that would have frozen a polar bear's testicles.

Feeling somewhat sheepish Carson led the way, pushing the stolen pistol into his belt. He held the rifle loosely while anxiously glancing over his shoulder. A wave of giddiness swept over him.

The pounding he had received from his fight in the arena had weakened him more than he had imagined. For a moment he had to lean against a tree trunk.

While he was resting he noticed a polished piece of hickory standing upright in the earth. With a grunt of satisfaction he picked up a long-handled axe. It had evidently been used for chopping wood. Examining his find he was quite pleased with his new weapon.

'What have you got there?'

Carson looked up with a slight smile on his face.

'An axe.'

He was swinging the axe to get the feel of the balance as Henrietta emerged from the line of ponies and signalled urgently to him.

14

They selected their ponies and found saddles underneath a tarpaulin. All the time as they worked they expected an alarm to be raised. However they accomplished the saddling up without incident and walked their mounts away from the camp. Once well down the trail they swung onto the horses.

Diego grinned at his companions.

'The God above watches over us.'

Carson slung his new axe on his saddle. He thought it prudent to keep the carbine ready until they were well away from the bandits' encampment.

'It may not be long before they find we are gone. They will be after us with a vengeance. My guess is that they will expect us to head south to the border. I suggest we head west. Tomorrow we can plan a route south.'

'I know these parts well. I can guide

you to safety,' interposed the new recruit.

Far into the night they rode, wary of any lights, which would indicate dwellings. They passed like ghosts, riding quietly, hoping that no one observed them on their journey.

Keeping to a steady trot the miles dropped behind them. As they rode, the loneliness of the night crept upon them. The terrain was rising gradually and sometime in the night their horses were treading over a steep incline. During the day temperatures soared till they were uncomfortably hot. Now in the night the opposite occurred and the temperature plummeted.

No one spoke as they hunched deep inside their clothes against the keen northeast wind that blew remorselessly with a sharpness that cut through their thin garments.

The horses moved steadily onwards with hardly any guidance from their riders. They were like dark wraiths against the bright moonlight.

When the dawn came it edged into their perception with a silver-grey brightness. The wind brought with it flurries of dust. Temperatures began to rise imperceptibly. With the sunrise they were able to take note of their surroundings.

'Where are we?' asked Carson.

'We're in the Crate Hills.'

Diego pointed to a glint of water just visible.

'A string of lakes run along in the general direction we want to go.'

He shivered in the chill wind that blew relentlessly across the hills.

'We need shelter and food. Perhaps we'll come on a dwelling soon.'

Even as he spoke they saw the huddle of buildings nestling in a shallow depression. It was a natural place to build in this exposed landscape. The dip in the land would give some shelter. They studied the place for a few moments. There seemed to be no sign of activity. As one they turned their mounts and plodded down towards the buildings.

'Help, please help me!'

The sudden hollering out of the quiet dawn startled them for they could see no one about. They looked around for the source of the voice.

'Help, over here, over here.'

There was some agitated movement in the centre of a cultivated field. They reined in and stared hard across the plot of corn. The calls were coming from a figure in the middle of the field. The man was wriggling about but was restrained in some manner.

'What'd you think?'

'One of us could go and see.'

Carson slid from his mount. His legs were stiff and ached somewhat from the long hours in the saddle. He carried the carbine with him on his walk across the field. As he drew closer the man called out.

'Thank God, you've come.'

Carson saw why the man had been calling for help. A crude cross had been erected in the field. The man was tethered to this makeshift crucifix. Carson blinked in surprise, remembering his own captivity in the ancient chapel back at the Place of Holy Bones. Around the man's neck was a dog collar.

'May the Lord be praised for your timely arrival.'

Carson could see the man was shivering violently from exposure to the chilly wind.

'What's going on, Reverend?'

'Damn hussies! Just release me and I'll explain everything.'

Carson started forward.

'What happened?'

Before the man could answer a shot whined overhead. Quickly Carson ducked behind the crucifix. He surmised the shot had come from the farm buildings.

'Murdering bastards!' the man behind whom he was sheltering screamed. 'Spawn of Satan! Whores of Babylon!'

Carson glanced towards his companions.

'Damnation!'

They still sat on their horses staring across at him, only their hands were not holding the reins anymore. Instead they held them locked on top of their heads. Four armed figures stood around them in a semicircle. Their rifles pointed up at the two riders.

'You there by the cross — throw down your weapons. We'll kill your two companions if you don't.'

It was a woman's voice and it came from the group of buildings towards which they had been heading.

'Take no notice of her. Cut me down. Do it quickly!'

The rifle blasted again. This time the bullet ploughed into the earth about a yard from Carson.

'All right, stop shooting,' he yelled back. 'I'll do what you want.'

His handgun was in his belt where it was hidden by his jacket. He grasped the carbine with both hands and held it aloft. Cautiously he stepped out from the cover of the crucifix, half expecting another shot and ready to duck back behind the crucified man. In full view of the marksman he tossed the weapon to the ground.

'Blast you to hell, you cowardly bastard!'

'Now, now, Reverend, that's no way for a man of God to speak,' Carson admonished mildly.

'Jesus Christ, my saviour, blast these devilish whores to hell, where they belong.'

'Who are these people you curse so vividly?'

'Whores, my friend — whores and sinners! The good Lord sent me to rescue them from their sinful ways. But Satan is strong in them and they overwhelmed me and exposed me to shame in this field — the field of Golgotha. Release me, my friend and God will reward you . . . '

The woman's voice called out again interrupting the man's pleas.

'Walk over here, slow and careful. If you make a move to release that evil creature the next bullet will be in your guts.'

'I'll come back for you, Reverend. Just keep up that praying for us.'

A string of curses followed him as he walked slowly across the field.

15

Everything about the homestead looked in good repair. There was a large single storied log building flanked by stables and barns. The woman that led Diego and Henrietta into the yard looked enormous in her yellow slicker.

Carson looked at the others escorting his companions. He was mildly surprised to see they were all female. One was middle-aged while the other two were no more than children. All carried the same determined expression. The rifles they held were steady and he noted the fingers curled firmly upon the triggers.

'Get down.'

Diego and Henrietta dismounted.

'Sandra.'

The big woman never took her eyes off Carson as she called out. In answer to her summons another woman appeared from around the corner of the house. Carson stared. He could see she was stunningly beautiful. He guessed she had been the one shooting at him in the field. Dark eyes stared bleakly back at him.

'What's going on here?' he demanded. 'Why are you harassing us like this? We were just passing through when we saw that preacher fellow. Thought we might be able to help.'

'All right, Libby, I'll take over now.'

The big woman nodded and backed away from Carson and his companions. The beauty called Sandra stared steadily at Carson.

'Right, big fella, as you can see we are suspicious of strangers around here. We don't get many travellers out this way. So start talking and tell me who you are, why you're here and where you're going.'

Carson considered the situation. For a brief moment he contemplated jumping the woman. He didn't know what sort of fighters they might be.

Certainly they seemed capable enough. They had seized the poor preacher and hung him out in the field.

He didn't think he could get to her before she or one of her companions shot him. There were five weapons in the yard, all held by five very determined females.

'Yes, I can see you wondering if you could get me before I can get a shot off at you. Before you get yourself killed I can reassure you we are all crack shots here. We are capable of downing all three of you where you stand.'

Carson slowly relaxed as he took in what the woman said.

'We don't mean no harm,' he said. 'We're only riding through.'

He glanced round at his companions. It was only then he noted Henrietta was hollow-eyed with weariness. She was leaning against her horse and her head drooped despondently. For the first time he felt the tiredness creep over him and realized the young girl could not carry on much longer without a break.

She needed food and shelter and rest, as did both Diego and himself. He had been so engrossed in putting as much distance as possible between themselves and the bandits he had given no thought to the consequences of pushing on all night without a break.

During his stint with the rangers he had worked under conditions like this and worse. Hardship and long rides were just tough situations to be endured and overcome. But even he with his enormous reserves of stamina was beginning to wilt. The punishing bout with the killer Gondor had been a gruelling affair and his body had not yet recovered from the battering.

He turned back to the woman. Somehow he had to negotiate with this fine-looking rifle-woman and obtain temporary shelter for his little group. Perhaps they had run far enough to be safe from General Rodriguez.

He looked at the disturbing woman whose rifle was still aimed steadily at his head. He decided he had nothing to lose by being completely honest with her. They were caught here — helplessly trapped by weariness and hunger as much as by these very capable women.

'We're fugitives — on the run,' he said simply. 'I don't know how much you know of a bandit who calls himself General Rodriguez. He's holed up at the Place of the Holy Bones. He was holding us prisoner but we managed to escape. All we ask for is food and rest then we'll be on our way.'

For long moments the woman stared at Carson. Slowly her gaze slid past him and took in Diego and Henrietta. Her eyes flicked back to Carson.

'Why was Rodriguez holding you prisoner?'

Carson wanted to lie — wanted to make up some fantastic tale that he thought the woman might believe. But he was too tired to think of anything.

'I'm a ranger assigned to caring for this young woman. We were attacked and taken prisoner by Rodriguez. He forced me to fight his champion Gondor.'

'You fought Gondor and lived!'

The woman's surprise was obvious. Carson smiled wryly.

'And not only did you live to tell about it but you then escaped from General Rodriguez.'

Slowly the rifle nozzle lowered.

'Well, who am I to deny hospitality to the man who defeated Gondor.'

She leaned closer and stared hard at Carson.

'It must have been a close thing. Your face looks a mess. Did you finish him?'

'Yeah,' Carson answered. 'I figured it was kill or be killed. Lucky for me Gondor was the one left lying in the dust.'

The tension in the little group seemed to ease considerably. Sandra looked around at her companions.

'What do you think? Is he telling the truth?'

The big woman Libby nodded.

'I think he is. No one would think

up a brainless story about defeating Gondor without some truth in it. If he's an enemy of General Rodriguez then he's a friend of ours.'

Guns were cautiously lowered and the women visibly relaxed. They were eyeing the little band of travellers with something akin to friendliness now.

'Take your horses in there.'

They were directed to the stables. Having tended to their tired mounts the equally tired humans were escorted to the house and everyone crowded into the large ranch house kitchen.

'Vegetable stew and potatoes OK with you?'

The smell of the stew pot gently simmering on the stove filled the kitchen with appetizing scents. To the hungry fugitives the reek of the cooking food was almost too much for their starving senses.

'I just hope there's enough to go around, *amigos*,' observed Diego who up till then had been uncharacteristically quiet.

And suddenly everyone was laughing. The two young girls were giggling. Sandra was smiling broadly as she ladled out bowls of the steaming mess.

While the guests seated themselves around the big table that took up most of the centre of the kitchen, Libby was placing fresh baked bread on the wooden surface.

'Eat up all you want. There's plenty to go around and then some. The number of bowls is unlimited. If it's eating competition you want, Libby holds the record with a total of five bowls at one sitting.'

Libby grinned proudly and putting her hands under her massive breasts began to jiggle them up and down.

'I'm a big woman with big appetites.'

She looked suggestively at Diego as she spoke. By now the kitchen was in an uproar. Hardly anyone could eat for laughing.

Sandra slid into the seat beside Carson.

'What about you, big man?' she said.

'Do you think you could handle Libby?'

Carson choked on his next mouthful. He grew red in the face and launched into a coughing fit. Libby came behind him and began to pound him on the back. She was smacking him so hard that the young ranger had great difficulty keeping his head out of his bowl of stew.

There was no holding back now. The kitchen echoed with laughter.

In the midst of all this hilarity Henrietta tried to keep an aloof calm. But even she had to cover her mouth in an attempt to stifle the infectious laughter bubbling up all around her.

During a lull in the mirth Carson recovered enough to make an attempt to divert attention away from his embarrassment.

'The guy out in the field . . . the preacher fella tied to the cross . . . what was all that about?'

If he had produced his revolver and loosed off a round he could not have brought about a more dramatic effect.

The laughter died amongst the women and they exchanged glances among each other. Silence hung heavy like a cloak of embarrassment as they bent their heads to the dishes on the table.

16

'He's no preacher — at least not as far as his actions are concerned,' Sandra said at last breaking the silence. 'A few days ago he came by here with Lisa and Tessie. They are twin sisters.'

She indicated the girls at the end of the table. They kept their heads lowered, their long hair hiding their faces.

'He is their father but in fact he claimed they were his handmaidens sent by a divine providence to minister to him. When he realized that Libby, Anna and me were on our own here on the farm he showed his true colours.'

Sandra paused and sipped a mouthful of stew before continuing.

'He preys on women and he thought he had an ideal situation here — three females with no men. In a very crude manner he tried to seduce me, claiming he had heard the voice of God commanding him to plant his seed in my loins. When I rebuffed him he grew nasty and tried to force himself on me. Well, he picked the wrong female to impregnate.'

Suddenly she looked up and stared defiantly at the mix of people around the table.

'He battered me some but I got the best of him. Laid him out cold and while he was unconscious I tied him up. Then I called Libby and Anna. We held a conference to decide what to do about him. At first I was in favour of setting him and his female companions back on the road and telling them to get the hell out of our lives. That was when we learned the true relationship of the so-called handmaidens.'

For a moment she tapped her spoon against the side of her dish — the sound somehow like a church bell — a church bell warning of mysteries not to be understood by ordinary humans.

'They told us they were his daughters

and for years he had been abusing them. When they saw him lying there trussed up like a lamb for the slaughter something burst within them. First one came forward and spat on him and the other quickly followed. Then they started to kick their helpless father. We had a job to pull them off.' At that point she smiled wryly. 'We held a mock trial then. Libby was appointed judge.'

The silence in the kitchen was intense as her guests listened raptly to her tale. No one was eating anymore — spoons suspended by the dishes while they waited for the remainder of the story to be told.

'We delayed till he recovered con-sciousness before proceeding. The twins gave evidence. I will not distress you by repeating their harrowing experiences. Here was a man steeped in the vilest of abusive behaviour made even more horrible by the fact that he was committing incest. While they spoke against him he cursed them and promised a terrible vengeance when he had them back in his power again.'

Sandra paused and contemplated the people around the table. All stared fixedly at her. Her eyes landed on Libby who nodded encouragingly.

'He was found guilty of gross behaviour, attempted rape, sacrilege and impersonating a preacher.'

Unexpectedly Sandra began to giggle. 'We couldn't think of any more charges.'

The tension around the table eased somewhat. Sandra recovered and continued her story.

'Libby made us all stand. She told us to rise while the verdict was announced. Reverend No-Shame she called him. She had obtained a black cap from somewhere and she solemnly placed this on her head and pronounced the death sentence.'

There was a scraping sound as Libby stood up. She bowed to the assembly.

'Reverend No-Shame,' she intoned. 'I sentence you to be taken from this place and put to death in a manner befitting that of a beast.'

Bowing again the big woman sat down again. There was a hushed silence as her audience sat pondering on all they had heard.

'You mean you're going to execute him?' Carson asked.

Sandra smiled wryly.

'You bet. But when it came to it none of us could bring ourselves to do it. So we tied him to that cross in the field where you found him. We thought it was right to hang him on a cross like the God he presumed to follow. When he is weak from hunger and exposure we are going to take him as far away as possible and loose him to fend for himself.'

The silence grew. Slowly the diners returned to the bowls of stew in front of them. No one spoke for a few moments — all of them concentrating on the food on the table. At last the middle-aged woman, Anna, who had helped the twins to take Diego and Henrietta captive, spoke up.

'Never mind Reverend No-Shame, what about these newcomers? Surely someone must be following them. From what I know of General Rodriguez he doesn't forgive easily and if what these people have said is true then his men will be coming after them.'

An ominous silence fell upon the assembly.

'Anna's right,' Sandra observed. She looked steadily at Carson. 'If that is the truth of the matter then you will bring even more trouble upon us. All we ever wanted was a quiet life.'

'Don't worry,' Carson assured her, 'no one will find us. We travelled all night. It would be sheer fluke if someone picked up our trail.'

At that moment the kitchen door slowly opened. All eyes turned towards the sound of the creaking hinges. Through the opening stepped a figure from hell.

17

The intruder was pointing a large revolver at the diners. An evil grin was fixed on his face and his eyes glittered fanatically as he waved the gun around the seated assembly. His dog collar left no one in any doubt as to his identity.

'Stay seated, brethren, we have more guests for dinner.'

Into the room filed half a dozen armed men. For moments the seated diners stared in confusion at this totally unwelcome and unexpected interruption.

'See, my friends, what did I tell you — a plentiful supply of women — more than enough to go round.'

Slowly walking along the table the demented preacher reached the far end where his two daughters sat. He reached out and gripped Lisa by her long tresses and savagely pulled her head back. The young girl gasped but made no other sound.

'These two I would recommend. I have personally sampled the delights of these little harlots. You'll forget who your mother is after a session with them.'

The bandits spread themselves around the room. In their eyes was a familiar hunger. Some licked their lips as they anticipated the entertainment to come.

Seated at the table, Carson was watching the men. He had been facing the door when it opened to their unwelcome visitors. Concealed by the table he had taken out his Colt. The odds were not good. The bandits were all armed. They had obviously given the preacher the gun after releasing him and he obligingly had led them to the farmhouse and the fugitives.

The preacher moved away from his daughters and moved up the table and stopped in front of Sandra.

'This one I reserve for myself. She

and I have a special relationship.'

The gun lashed out and hit Sandra across the forehead. Her head snapped back and blood began to leak down her face. In spite of the injury she stared defiantly up at her assailant.

'Bastard!'

The sudden scraping of a chair sounded loud in the tense room. Heads and weapons swivelled towards the sound. Libby was on her feet. Gun muzzles were raised to cover the big woman.

'Hey, you guys, what about me? What has a girl got to do to get some attention around here?'

Libby's hands were on the buttons of her blouse and she was rapidly unbuttoning. As she worked she was advancing towards the gunmen. The garment came free and Libby thrust her breasts at the men. They shifted and glanced bemusedly at each other. One of the bandits guffawed nervously. Several things happened then.

Sandra brought up a knife and slashed

it across the preacher's gun hand. The preacher cursed and dropped his weapon. At the same time Libby flung herself upon the nearest two gunmen and grappled with them. She was so close before launching her attack that neither of them had room to bring their weapons up. Carson brought up his own gun and fired at the remaining gunmen.

The noise of the shots was deafening in the confined space of the kitchen. His first shot punched a small hole in the forehead of the nearest bandit. The man's head crashed against the wall in a welter of blood and brains.

At the same time Carson fired he heard another gun firing as Henrietta opened up with her own revolver. Carson's second shot hit the next man in the shoulder and as the bandit swung around he managed to loose off a shot that buried itself harmlessly in the rear wall. Carson could not tell if Henrietta's shots were effective or not. He kept on shooting knowing he could not miss at such short range.

All hell broke loose. One of the bandits managed to bring up his weapon and started to trigger his revolver as the shots from Henrietta peppered his chest. The man spun round and his last shots sprayed into the fireplace.

Diego launched himself across the table and crashed into the men battling with Libby. A hail of bowls and dishes rained down on those of the gunmen trying to bring their weapons into play as Anna and the twins emptied the shelves of a large dresser for missiles.

The noise of firing was deafening. Smoke from the discharging weapons swirled in the air adding a pungent smell to the food-laden odours in the confines of the kitchen.

Sandra was on the floor wrestling with the preacher. Diego and Libby had selected a target each and were relentlessly battering their victims into submission. Carson and Henrietta fired simultaneously at the last gunman.

As the bullets hit home the gunman

crashed back with thick gouts of blood splattering the wall behind him. Carson kicked himself free of the table and chairs and rolled across the table and on to the preacher. He used his gun to bludgeon the man. The preacher tried to turn on his new attacker but Carson clubbed him again and with a groan the holy man subsided.

A sudden quiet descended on the room. The bodies of the slain bandits lay crumpled against one wall. Diego and Libby stood panting triumphantly astride their bruised and battered opponents. Carson stared at Sandra now sitting on the floor with a large cut on her forehead and blood leaking from her nose. He reached out and helped her to her feet.

'You hurt bad?' he asked her.

'No, I'm OK.'

'You look awful.'

She grinned back at him.

'Not quite as bad as you, yet. I'd have to go a few more rounds with the preacher to equal your looks.'

As she spoke she looked down and kicked viciously at the man lying on the floor.

Carson glanced around him, trying to assess the damage. The fumes of cordite still hung in the room. Chairs were overturned and smashed crockery littered the floor and table. Suddenly everyone was talking at once. Excitement and hysteria was in the air.

Libby hugged Diego and thanked him for coming to her assistance. The twins and Anne were laughingly re-enacting their crockery barrage. Henrietta still sat at the table staring around at the carnage. He felt a light touch on his arm and turned to look down at Sandra. She was smiling wearily at him.

'It looks as if we survived.'

Carson relaxed. It was true. Their motley little band of men and women had survived against all odds.

The band of armed men had come suddenly upon them as they sat eating and yet now some of the intruders lay dead while those that remained were rendered helpless. A sudden thought struck him. He moved to stand before the groaning figure of Libby's victim.

'How did you find us?' he asked.

The man stared back at him with naked hatred. 'Go to hell!'

Carson's boot smashed into the man's groin. The gunman curled up in agony. The young ranger crouched beside the injured man and gripping him by the hair jerked him into a sitting position.

'There are two ways to do this, my friend. I've just showed you the friendly way. There are more unfriendly ways of extracting information. I'll pretend I wasn't so friendly that time and we'll try again.'

Before the man could answer the sound of a shot from somewhere outside and the smashing of glass as a window erupted postponed further interrogation.

'Hello, you in the house! What's happening in there?' After a short pause the voice continued. 'Pedro, are you in there? What's happening?'

The man whom Carson had been interrogating suddenly screamed out, 'Gonzales, they've got us. Come and kill the bastards!'

18

Carson's fist slammed into the side of the man's head and his shouts were abruptly cut off. But the damage had been done. It was the signal the men outside awaited.

A thunderous hail of fire and the disintegration of all the windows in the front of the building followed. The people in the big kitchen cowered down covering their heads with their arms. Along with the bullets pouring into the house, lethal splinters of wood and glass swept across the room forming a deadly hail.

Carson crawled to the window picking up an abandoned weapon and raising his arm without lifting himself from the floor managed to empty the revolver towards the unseen enemy. He knew the gesture was futile but it might give the attackers pause in case they

were thinking of following up their
volley with a rush into the house.
The women, spurred on by Carson's
example, crawled to the windows and
began firing.

'Diego,' Carson called in a lull
between the firing, 'make sure none of
the prisoners can get loose.'

Obediently Diego, with his helper,
Libby, pushed and bullied the wounded
men into a side pantry and blocked the
door with a chair. This had to be done
entirely on all fours, as the sporadic vol-
leys from outside the house continued.

'Where's the reverend?' Sandra suddenly shouted above the noise of
splintering wood and glass and gunfire.

Carson, using a rifle taken from one
of the dead bandits, had been risking
a peek outside and firing at likely
targets. His gaze swept around the
room. Except for its original occupants
and the dead bandits there was no sign
of the Reverend No-Shame.

'Forget about him, try and get a shot
out of the windows if you can.'

He fired off a burst, dropped to the floor and elbowed his way across to Sandra. She was lying by the door firing through one of the panels that had disintegrated in the attack. He put his mouth close to her ear.

'This isn't your fight. We should try and negotiate a surrender and safe passage for you and your companions.'

For answer she turned to face him and to his surprise kissed him full on the mouth.

'You're a lovely man, Mr. Carson, but utterly naïve.'

He stared confused back at her and for a wild moment wished she would kiss him again. She had blood on her face and her hair was in disarray. Her clothes were dusty and torn from her brawl with the preacher yet he had never seen anyone so desirable. Seeing his bewilderment she grinned.

'You saw the look on those men's faces when the preacher brought them inside and told them there were plenty of women to go around. Do you think those men outside are any different?'

'But,' he interrupted, 'it's us they want . . . '

This time it was her finger on his lips that silenced him.

'Hush, we've been through all this before — bands of men roaming through and wanting to make sport with us. Why do you think we're so cautious and so well armed?'

She turned and fired a few more rounds through the splintered panel.

'Ask any of the women. I know I speak for Anna and Libby. They'd want to fight on. I can't speak for the twins. But after their experiences with their own father I doubt if they would want to be back in his power again.'

Carson cocked his head to one side and after listening for a moment held up his hand.

'Stop firing!' he yelled.

The people in the kitchen had been poking weapons out of windows and loosing off without really seeing anything. Carson had to yell again before they took any notice of him. One by one they ceased their shooting and turned to stare at him. An eerie silence hung around the place. It was only when they quit their own firing that they realized the enemy had ceased also.

Now the defenders squatted on the floor of the kitchen and listened. The silence was tangible after the intensity of the gunfire. The besieged group sat there dazed and somewhat shell-shocked after the furious violence and intensity of the gunfire.

'Anna.'

Libby was suddenly crawling to the still figure lying beyond the table. The big woman reached out and touched the sprawled figure. While the others watched, Libby gently touched Anna's face and then the big woman issued a low moan.

'Anna . . . Anna . . .'

Then a voice was shouting from outside, startling them all. Carson swung round and cautiously peered around the ruined window frame. A white rag tied to a pole was jigging from behind one of the outbuildings.

'Hello, the house.'

Without exposing himself Carson yelled back. 'Yeah, what do you want?'

'Can someone talk to us?'

'Why?'

'We don't want anyone hurt. We can parley.'

Carson turned back to the room.

'I think we'd better talk. Perhaps I can negotiate a safe way out of this.'

He stood up.

'All right, I'm coming out,' he yelled. 'Don't do anything stupid. We still have some of your men here.'

Sandra was suddenly beside him.

'Don't go. Let me go instead. After all it's my land they're trespassing on.'

Carson reached behind him and shoved his pistol into his waistband. He adjusted his jacket to cover the weapon.

'Don't worry about me. They'll be more likely to take notice of a man.'

He looked over at Libby still kneeling

152

beside the body of Anna.

'I'm sorry about Anna. I'll do my best to get you out of here.'

Carson wrenched open the ruined door and stepped outside.

19

As soon as Carson appeared in the yard the figure of a man moved into sight. He carried a fence rail on which hung a white shirt. Slowly the young ranger walked forward and the man with the makeshift flag did likewise. They stopped when about twenty feet separated them. Carson faced a man almost as tall as himself but without his own muscular build. He had jet-black hair swept back from his forehead. His face was narrow and shrewd.

'You Gonzales?'

The man nodded.

'You want to save yourself, give up now. I'll take you back and General Rodriguez will let you join up with him.'

'Sorry, friend, but we outnumber you. And we're in good cover. We outgun you.'

'I know just who's in there, Carson. The preacher — he tells me there are just a few women and a couple of beat-up vagrants.'

Carson cursed.

'He would tell you that. We rescued his concubines from him.'

The raised eyebrows of the man indicated he was unaware of the reverend's reputation.

'The man's an evil bastard. He's no more a preacher than you or I. The concubines I am referring to are his daughters. There are one or two women inside but he wants them for his own use. We have more than enough men to hold you off and inflict more casualties.'

'*No importa*, Carson, you and Senorita Henrietta surrender and I'll let the rest go. If you behave yourself and comply with my instructions I'll even kill the preacher for you.' The bandit shrugged expressively. '*Sta bueno?*'

Carson stared back at the man.

'I'll have to consult with the others. My belief is they will want to fight on.'

'*Por el amor de Dios*, Carson. You make things very difficult. My orders are to bring back Senorita Henrietta. I couldn't care less what happens to the rest of you. Hand over the girl and you can go free. I was to bring you in also but I can always say you were killed when we rescued the girl. And,' the bandit smiled wryly, 'even a girl can die in crossfire. What do you say? Save yourself a lot of grief — eh?'

Carson hesitated. Henrietta would come to no actual harm if she returned, whereas she was in real danger of being killed or seriously injured if she remained in the ranch house. Already one woman lay dead.

'You'll be the one in trouble if you happen to hurt the girl. General Rodriguez won't like that one little bit. In fact he'll be very angry.'

The bandit shrugged.

'These hills are alive with bands of Injuns. Who is to say they attacked your little party and wiped you out. We came upon the scene of the massacre. Madre

Dios, no one left to tell the tale. There was nothing I could do. General Rodriguez can't blame me for that.'

Carson could sense the bandit meant every word. If the girl died he could simply kill everyone involved so that his version of events would be the only one heard. His men would follow orders and back up his story — for their leader's guilt would be theirs and his punishment for failure would be theirs also.

'I can't decide this on my own. I have to consult with the others.'

'*Sí*, Senor Carson, I'll give you ten minutes.'

'My advice to you, friend, is to ride away from here. I promise you'll be the ones to die, not us.'

The bandit smiled.

'Ten minutes, Carson, I'll be fair and not start counting until you have re-entered the house. *Quien sabe*?'

For a few moments the two men stared at each other trying to gauge the other's resolution. The bandit tucked his makeshift flag of truce under his arm and slowly backed away.

Carson turned and strode back to the farmhouse.

Sandra had been busy while Carson was outside. The large dining table had been overturned and as soon as the big man was inside it was pushed against the bullet-riddled door. Anna's body had been taken into an adjoining room. An anxious group faced him as he told them all that had been said.

'The bottom line is if he gets me and Henrietta then the rest go free. He even promised to let me escape.'

'Then there's no option.' Henrietta looked around at her companions. 'Thank you for all you've done.'

She crossed to the door.

Diego stepped in her way. The girl smiled at him.

'I have to go out there. I have no right to cower behind innocent people.'

Carson moved to stand beside Diego. Suddenly Libby joined Diego then Sandra moved into the line and sheepishly the twins followed suit. Henrietta stared at the line of bodies barring her progress to the door.

'You . . . you can't do this,' the girl appealed to them. 'It's stupid and pointless. I go outside, give myself over to those people and you are free and safe. They only want me as a hostage to force my father to pay for my safety. They won't harm me. I'm no use to them dead. So will you please move aside and let me through.'

Sandra was staring at the girl.

'What do you mean?'

'I suppose we should have told you but somehow the opportunity never arose. I'm Henrietta Xavier. My father is one of the richest and most influential men in Mexico. Carson's ranger company were escorting me to my home when General Rodriguez captured us. Once General Rodriguez has me in his power he can force my father to help him take over the government of Mexico.'

20

The silence grew as the little assembly took all this in. Libby was the first to speak.

'We're not letting you out there on your own. I for one will fight on to protect you.'

One by one the others, following Libby's lead, vowed to protect the girl. She in turn stared hard at these bedraggled volunteers.

'It's not necessary,' she whispered, 'I will go to General Rodriguez — you will go your separate ways in peace and safety. Now let me go outside.'

For a moment no one moved, then Carson spoke out.

'When I wanted to go into the camp and seek out Rodriguez and kill him you reminded me I had taken an oath to protect the people of Texas. I would not be faithful to that oath if I allowed you to go out there. My duty is to protect you and that's what I'll do.'

'Anyway, what guarantee have we that once the bandits have you they will ride away and leave us alone,' interjected Sandra. 'We had men once on this farm to protect us. I had a husband. One day a party of bandits just like the ones out there rode up and took our men. They were recruiting for fighters.

'Later they came back, for they knew we were alone. Anna's husband had not been taken, as he was considered too old. He tried to defend us. We fought too, but there were just too many . . . '

A voice from outside interrupted Sandra's narrative.

'Five minutes!'

'Is there a back way out?' asked Diego. 'We could maybe escape that way.'

Sandra shook her head.

'We boarded everything up thinking we would only have to defend one front. We never envisioned anything like this.'

'You say you boarded it up. Couldn't we undo that? Wait for nightfall and then make a break for it. What tools have you?'

'All the tools are out in the barns. But there are all the kitchen bits and pieces.'

'Diego, take one of the twins with you. Start making an exit hole — break through a door or window, whichever is easiest. But be quiet about it. They mustn't know what we're planning.'

The shot when it came startled them all.

'Your time's up! Just come out one by one with your hands in the air.'

Carson strode to the window.

'Ride off,' he yelled, 'while you and your men still can.'

He fired his weapon out into the yard to emphasize his challenge.

The hail of bullets when it came seemed more intense and violent than that previously experienced. The remnants of crockery left on the dresser exploded and scattered on the floor. No one could stand up. All they could do was poke weapons through a ruined window or door, pull the trigger and hope they were doing enough to keep the attackers at bay.

The noise was deafening. Gun fumes along with debris from the disintegrating surroundings filled the room in a dust-laden haze. Occasionally there would be a break in the firing and a voice would call on them to surrender.

'How long can they keep up this barrage?' Henrietta asked Carson during one of these lulls.

The youngster shrugged.

'They seem to have plenty of ammo and perhaps they are waiting for reinforcements. They would have sent someone back to the main camp. In that case they can afford to waste ammunition. I just hope the reinforcements don't arrive before nightfall. It's going to be tough enough to get out without extra men patrolling around the place.'

The fusillade resumed. Carson sighted

through a hole in the door and fired out into the yard. It was impossible to tell if the defenders' shooting was effective. It was not safe to linger after firing. Loose off a shot, roll or crawl to another gaping hole and fire again.

The room was a surreal scene from a hellish nightmare. Acrid smoke and dust clouded the atmosphere. Dim figures shifted about the room seeking a hole to fire through. Except for the occasional interlude in the barrage it was impossible to hold a conversation.

The defenders moved around like lost souls in hell, doomed for eternity to dwell in fume-filled rooms and endlessly discharge guns towards a hidden enemy. Clothes, faces and hands quickly became dusty from rolling around on the debris littered floor. Garments tore on splinters from the disintegrating walls and furniture.

Carson wondered if the course they had adopted was the wisest one. He looked across at Henrietta and noticed her begrimed and filthy condition. She seemed tireless in her efforts to defend the house — shooting — shifting her position — shooting. It was as if by her personal efforts she had to extricate them from this situation and was working harder than anyone else to do so.

Sandra grinned at him, showing startlingly white teeth in her dirty face before firing again. Libby fired and rolled and fired again. Because of her size she never stood or crawled — just rolled from one vantage point to another.

Tessie seemed to be staying put. She was still firing her rifle but was not moving about, as were the others. Something stung Carson on the shoulder. He dropped flat and craned his neck to see what had happened. A crimson streak began to spread on his shirt. He swore silently. How much more of this could they take.

He crawled over to Tessie. She turned a drained face to him and tried a smile. He saw the dark stain down the side of her blouse.

'Christ, you're hit, girl. Let me see.'

The girl shook her head in dismissal.

'I'm fine,' she mouthed, her words inaudible in the hellish din.

Carson was about to insist when he realized the delicate nature of the girl's wound. He yelled at Sandra, trying to attract her attention. She crawled over. Carson indicated his own chest and then pointed at the girl.

21

Tessie tried to brush aside Sandra's attentions. The woman insisted the girl lie back. The side of the wounded girl's blouse was stained a dark red. Carson left them and crawled back to the splintered door.

He saw Libby jerk back and press a hand to her ear. When she took her hand away her fingers were covered in blood.

He felt a dread well up in him — not for himself but for all these women resisting so valiantly. This was not fighting, as he knew it. The defenders were helpless targets, penned-up as they were. Desperately he wracked his brain for a solution. Nothing came readily to mind. He realized the only course open to him was to persuade the women to give up.

There was only one way out and that

was to surrender to the bandits and hope they would allow some of them to get away as promised. Either that or hold on until night and risk an escape through the back of the house.

Ruefully he wondered how many of them would be able to walk under their own steam by then. He fired again and again in an angry burst, despair weighing on him and threatening to break his spirit. There was no place to go. For a moment he wished he were back in the arena with Gondor. At least back there he only had himself to worry about.

Someone was banging on his foot. He glanced behind and saw Diego lying flat on the floor and whacking on his boot with a wooden mallet.

Diego and the twin Lisa had gathered a miscellany of knives and forks and anything else that could be used for cutting and hacking and had been busy all morning back in one of the living rooms. In all the noise and confusion of the assault Carson had all but forgotten about them.

Diego was beckoning to him and Carson nodded, fired another burst and turned back to Diego. The young Mexican was reversing back through the door that led into the rear of the house. Carson squirmed along the floor after him, his bruised body painful and stiff as he used his arms to pull himself along. He followed Diego to a rear wall.

Lisa lay on the floor amidst a welter of shavings and chips of wood. She looked over at Carson and then pointed to a small opening hacked in the wall behind her. Carson nodded in approval. He crawled closer to Diego. The noise of the bombardment back here was muted but Diego still had to put his mouth to Carson's ear and shout.

'Venga! Something strange going on out there. Thought you might like to take a look. See what you can make of it.'

Cautiously Carson put his face to the crude hole and peered outside. There was a corral behind the house. He could see a few terrified goats huddled in one corner. Their mouths were opening and closing but no sound carried above the noise of the shooting taking place out front. Suddenly he tensed.

A head poked cautiously above the fence, then another and another till several heads could be seen. There was a sudden movement and a man vaulted over the fence. There was a flash of buckskin. Carson sucked in his breath. Another abrupt movement and another buckskin-clad figure joined the first.

The realization dawned on Carson. These were the reinforcements sent for by Gonzales. He raised his rifle and began to poke it through the opening. He felt a hand on his arm.

'Wait amigo, they're not Mexicans,' Diego yelled into his ear.

Carson examined the men invading the paddock. Dressed in buckskins there was nothing to suggest they were Mexican bandits. He was nonplussed by their behaviour. They strolled across the grass as if they were walking down the main street of their local town. Carson counted at least a dozen. He turned to Diego. But the man looked as puzzled as he did.

Carson shrugged resignedly. If these were reinforcements then they could not hope to win. The odds against them had suddenly risen in the bandits' favour.

On an impulse he reversed his position and with one powerful thrust of his feet burst a great hole in the wall weakened by Diego's efforts. He pushed his head and shoulders through the hole and stopped moving as he felt a small hard object pressing down on top of his head.

Cautiously he raised his head feeling the thing trace a line along his skull. The nozzle of the gun ended up resting against his forehead. A rough bearded face leered at him from behind the barrel of the weapon.

'Howdy, laddie, and where do you think you're going?'

Carson stared at the man.

'We want to surrender,' he croaked.

22

There was a chuckle that seemed to come from somewhere deep within the bowels of the bearded man.

'Dear me, and there was me thinking I had a fight on my hands. Charlie, inside with you. The rest of you men spread out. Don't expose yourselves till we've found out what's going on.'

A meaty hand pushed at Carson's face.

'You — back inside and stand well clear. Charlie here is coming in. Any tricks and I'll start shooting.'

A slim dark man with a wicked scar running the length of his face pushed inside the hole vacated by Carson. As he straightened up a rifle was pushed through to him. He glanced around the room, grinned, and moved away from the hole in the wall. Three more fighters followed the bearded man.

'Well now, what's this all about?'

'We've decided we've had enough. There's too many of you. With you in the game we know we don't stand a chance. Do the terms of the surrender still stand?'

'You tell me, laddie. What are the terms?'

For a moment Carson was nonplussed.

'Didn't Gonzales tell you what's happening?'

'And just who is Gonzales?'

Carson stared hard at the bearded, shrewd-eyed face. There was something he was not picking up on here. His eyes narrowed in concentration.

'Surely you're the reinforcements called up by Gonzales. He told us you were coming.'

'This Gonzales — tell me about him.'

'He's leading a band of General Rodriguez's men — they came after us — trapped us here . . . '

Carson trailed off, aware of a sudden tautness in the other man's face.

'Rodriguez — is that his men out front?'

It was Diego who voiced the suspicion that was forming in Carson's mind.

'You're not the reinforcements — you're trappers.'

The man turned and issued a stream of instructions through the hole in the wall. Suddenly men were clambering inside. The room rapidly became crowded with the fierce-looking warriors.

'I've sent men around both sides of the buildings to flank this Gonzales. Let's see if we can bloody him somewhat.'

From that moment events moved outside the besiegers' control.

Sandra stared in bewilderment as a buckskin-clad man appeared from nowhere, crouched beside her and began firing through the tattered door. Even more bewildering was the sight of more men taking up firing positions beside the remainder of Sandra's team.

The newcomers commenced to lay down a lethal field of fire to the front of the house. Stimulated by the sudden arrival of reinforcements the bemused defenders began firing with renewed enthusiasm. The noise of gunfire intensified.

Carson and Diego looked at each other, shrugged and went forward to join the fight. They had hardly taken up a firing position when at a signal from the bearded leader the upturned table was dragged back and booted feet kicked out the ruined door.

Fighters poured through the smashed doorway and some were even breaking out the remains of damaged windows and leaping into the yard.

Carson, unable to contain his excitement, grabbed his axe and plunged out after them. As he hurled himself in the wake of the trappers he became aware of the fierce screams they were emitting.

It was an awesome experience going into battle with these crazy warriors.

They never faltered in the face of the fire coming from the bandits. Yelling and screaming, they hurled themselves forward at the bandits firing into the farmhouse.

Men fell as the bandits kept on firing. Carson had to leap across a body as a man went down with a bullet in the head. Men staggered or stumbled as they were hit but others kept on running towards the enemy.

Carson felt the whizzing about his head of near misses. The bravery of the attacking force was infectious. This sudden activity was a welcome change from huddling in the house and being shot at. He emptied his pistol towards the enemy.

Gonzales must have realized he had been tricked for the trapper's frontal attack was reinforced by men firing into his flanks. The bandits quickly realized their untenable situation as they saw buckskin-clad warriors coming from every direction. Many of them turned to flee. It was one thing firing from cover at a static building defended by a few women but it was another thing altogether facing screaming maniacs who shot back.

Thrusting his empty pistol into his waistband and gripping his axe Carson screamed along with his companions. Almost as he brandished the weapon they were upon the opposing bandits.

23

A Mexican swung his rifle towards Carson. The blade of the axe hit the man on the shoulder and bowled him over. Carson kicked the man in the head as he went down. He was screaming out his anger and blood lust along with his battle-crazed companions.

Ahead of the young ranger a trapper was using his weapon as a cudgel trying to fend off an attacker. He slipped and went down. Before his opponent could brain him Carson stepped in and once more the fearsome axe did its work. Carson was getting used to the feel of the weapon. This time the sharp blade punched into the man's neck. There was a satisfying thud and the man went down in a spray of blood.

Carson kept on swinging at the enemy. He dealt out dreadful wounds with that terrible axe. Men went down before him as he screamed and lashed out. No one could stand against him. He was a man deranged by blood lust. The hatred he felt for the man he held responsible for the death of his grandfather had been bottled up while he was held prisoner. Now he could vent that hatred on Rodriguez's henchmen.

Suddenly he ran out of opposition. Carson glared wildly around him. In the distance he could see the remnants of the bandit force scrambling onto their horses and whipping them away from the scene of battle. He ached to give chase. The numbers he had killed and maimed in his frenzied, butchering spree did not satisfy the killing demon now aroused within him.

Breathing hard he looked behind him. A scene of carnage greeted him. Men lay sprawled across the spaces between the buildings. Firing had ceased. All that could be heard was the screams of the wounded and the cries for help.

'Jesus man, you're a holy terror with that axe.'

Carson looked at the man who spoke. It was the bearded trapper who had put the gun to his head at the back of the house. The men were gathering around their leader. Some were grinning at Carson.

'I'm glad you ended up on our side. I wouldn't fancy that thing embedded in my head.'

Carson looked down at his weapon. It was covered in blood and bits of flesh and hair. He noticed with some concern his forearms were also covered in red gore.

'It's only an axe,' he said vaguely.

A fierce-looking warrior walked up to him and stuck out his hand.

'Jim Middett,' he announced, 'thanks for saving me back there. I slipped on some blood. The booger had me till you put that axe in his neck. Hope I can return the favour some time.'

The bearded man who was obviously the leader looked appraisingly at Carson.

'You fight well.'

He looked around at the carnage.

'Middett, see to the wounded and gather any weapons lying around. Get someone to collect the stray horses.'

He gestured at Carson.

'Come on, let's get back to the house.'

The farmhouse had become an infirmary. Wounded men were propped against the walls or sprawled on chairs being attended to by the women. Sandra looked up as Carson and his companion entered the room. Her face was dirty with smudges of blood and her hair was dusty and unkempt but somehow she still managed to look attractive.

'You're hurt!' she exclaimed and crossed to Carson.

The youngster looked down at her and then down at himself. For the first time he began to wonder if some of the blood that spattered his person was indeed his.

'I'm OK,' he said uncertainly and

turned to the man beside him to distract from his confusion that seemed to overwhelm him every time the young woman came near him. 'This is . . . I don't know your name.'

The bearded man bowed slightly to Sandra.

'Ben is my name, Ben Black. Some call me Black Ben but my friends call me Ben.'

Sandra smiled.

'I'm Sandra and this fierce looking butcher is Carson.'

Looking around the room she named her companions to Black Ben.

'These are the people you've rescued.'

She turned back uncertainly to the bearded trapper.

'Are you . . . ' she paused uncertainly, 'are you — brigands?'

She looked embarrassed even as she spoke.

24

Black Ben laughed out loud, his teeth showing startlingly white against his dark beard.

'I've been called worse things than that. Usually I shoot the person that calls me so. But I'll forgive you as you have been under some strain.'

He waved around at his men.

'We're trappers.'

At that moment Middett poked his head in through the ruined doorway.

'Got about ten horses and all the arms.'

He held up a Winchester rifle.

'First class firing pieces — if we were all armed with weapons like these we could march on General Rodriguez and end his bloody gang within a week. Some of the bandits got away. They'll most likely bring back help.'

Black Ben nodded and looked

around at the wounded strewn about the room. There was a background noise of moans from the injured men. The women, assisted by one or two of the newcomers, were trying to cope with the wounded.

Basins of bloodied water used for washing wounds sat about on the floor. Crude pads and bandages were being made from towels and bed sheets. There was a strong smell of spirits as bottles of whiskey were passed around. The whiskey was being consumed by those who were able to swill it down and was also being used to swab out wounds and cuts.

'We'll have to leave shortly. Give the orders to the men to begin moving out.'

Black Ben turned to Carson.

'What are your plans?'

Carson shrugged. 'We have no option but to hide out somewhere. We were trying to make it to the border but when Rodriguez finds out we've eluded capture then the border will be watched. I never imagined they would catch up with us so quickly. They must have good trackers to have found us here.'

For a moment Black Ben frowned thoughtfully then his brow cleared as he came to some decision.

'Why don't you come with us? You can bunk with us for a while.'

He grinned at Carson with that engaging smile.

'You might even think of joining us. We need good strong fighters like yourself.'

Carson smiled back at his bearded rescuer.

'We do need a place to hide out till it's safe to go south. I would take up your offer of refuge, but I'll have to consult with my companions if they want to tag along with you.'

'Right, we leave in five minutes. Do what you have to in that time.'

The bearded leader turned to the room of wounded men and began organizing an evacuation.

Carson searched for Henrietta amongst

the confusion that was once a peaceful ranch house kitchen. He found her comforting a young fighter with half his face shot away. She was crouched down beside him holding his hand and talking softly. His one remaining eye stared unblinkingly up at her. Carson felt like an intruder as he touched her shoulder to draw her attention.

The girl turned a harrowed face towards him. Her eyes were filled with sadness. He glanced at the man she had been tending — a boy not much younger than he was himself. A bloodied pad was tied in place around his head but it did not hide the fact that most of that side of his face had been shot away.

'Henrietta, we have to leave soon. Black Ben has offered us refuge for a time with his people. We have to make a decision to accompany him or start out again on our own. I had thoughts to hide out with him for a while before trying to make it to the border again.'

'We have no option. Right now he's our only hope.'

In a surprisingly short time the whole band was on the move. Carson and his companions had recovered their mounts and rode in the wake of the trappers. The wounded were ferried along in an old wagon from the farm.

Henrietta rode beside Libby and Carson smiled at the difference in the size of the two women. Henrietta was small and dainty atop her mount while Libby's vast bulk looked out of place beside her. Sandra rode with Carson and he was very conscious of her presence.

The twins hung round Diego and Carson could see the young bandit was enjoying himself as he regaled them with tales of his adventures.

Carson had reasoned they were safer hiding out with Black Ben while the bandits hunted for them. Rodriguez would guess rightly the fugitives would head south in an attempt to reach Senor Xavier's estates. Hopefully as time went on and the searchers were unsuccessful their vigilance would diminish and he could then strike out for the border and safety.

He sighed deeply. His was a huge responsibility. From a humble ranger he seemed, by a set of unfortunate circumstances, to be appointed sole bodyguard to Henrietta.

So far he hadn't done so well. Now they were at the mercy of a band of trappers. He was not even sure he could trust Black Ben.

He sighed deeply, hardly aware of doing so, to be rewarded by a sudden smile from Sandra.

'You seem worried about something, Carson. What's bothering you?'

'I'm wondering how far we can trust Black Ben. I can't rid myself of this feeling we are leaping from a leaky boat onto an island that is about to be swamped by the tide.'

She edged her mount closer to him and her warm smile momentarily distracted him from his gloomy thoughts.

'I'm sure he's not as bad as you think. Why would he go to the bother of rescuing us just to do us harm? And anyway he seems to like you. He wants to recruit you into his band. You could do worse than join up with him.'

'Yeah, but I have more important things to do and maybe the only reason Black Ben rescued us was to wangle some profit from our situation.'

Again he sighed deeply. Then he felt Sandra's hand reach out and grip his arm. In spite of the nagging doubts about their rescuers, it was with a pleasant tingle in his body that he rode on to whatever fate awaited them.

25

The trapper's stronghold was a small group of log cabins surrounded by a wooden stockade. The inhabitants came out to greet the returning warriors. They took charge of the horses captured from Rodriguez's men as well as the cattle and goats that had belonged to Sandra and her company. The wounded were moved into the cabins to be cared for.

Carson and his party were billeted in a couple of small cabins whose sole inhabitants were two ancient crones. Sandra joined Carson along with Henrietta in one shack while Diego, Libby and the twins occupied another.

Only the light from a blazing log fire relieved the gloom of the interior of the cabin. While they sat before the cheery flames the old woman set about providing a simple meal for the travellers.

Carson quizzed the woman about life in the stockade. She told of Rodriguez's depredations into the various communities, killing and looting where he could.

'My husband and my two sons were killed during one such raid. My daughter was raped. She was only twelve at the time.'

The old woman spoke dispassionately.

'She survived and now she scouts for Black Ben. It was her as brought him news of parties of bandits out searching the countryside. Our men rode out to see if they could catch some of them in an ambush. By the amount of horses you brought back it looks as if they were successful.'

'Yes,' Carson rejoined, 'your men killed a great many bandits. They're a great bunch of fighters.'

The woman smiled back at him and he was not sure if her pleasure was for his compliment to the fighting abilities of Black Ben's men or the fact that they had successfully ambushed and killed so many bandits.

The old woman took Henrietta and Sandra to one side and showed them the sleeping arrangements. Curtains of buffalo hides partitioned off the rooms. The beds were simple straw-filled paliasses laid on the dirt floor.

Carson was happy to leave the sleeping arrangements to the women. He sat contentedly by the fire watching flames leap and spark in the chimney and was eventually joined by the womenfolk.

For a time they discussed the day's events but at last the old woman disappeared into the interior of the cabin to be shortly followed by Henrietta, leaving Carson and Sandra alone.

Carson watched the profile of Sandra as the firelight played upon her features. She turned and caught him watching her and smiled.

'Your thoughts or your wealth,' she challenged him. He grinned back at her.

'I was just thinking how pleasant this is — sitting before the fire with a full belly.'

Sandra laughed.

'Men. Give them a plate of stew and a hunk of bread and life is grand.'

'Not just that,' he said in a voice hesitant and shy. 'And a beautiful woman . . .'

He felt the blood surging into his cheeks as he spoke.

Sandra sat there smiling at him.

'I can see you're a real lady's man.'

She was leaning towards him. Awkwardly he reached out and somehow she was on his knee, her face close.

He slid his arms around her as her hands went around his neck. Her lips came down on his. As her lips pressed harder his excitement mounted. Sandra moaned as fire raced through her body. She bit hard on the lobe of his ear.

'Not here,' she breathed, 'we have our own private chamber.'

When she pulled away from him she looked into his eyes and saw the glaze of lust reflected there. Her own face was radiant from the hot flush of love that caroused through her. Somehow they prised themselves apart and stumbled to the sleeping quarters.

★   ★   ★

When Carson woke and felt the warm body snuggled against him he smiled contentedly and lay still, unwilling to wake his companion. For a moment he thought guiltily of all the things he should be doing. The seductive warmth of the lovely young woman in his berth was reason enough for the guilt to flit briefly across his mind like a butterfly choosing one tempting plant over another. He exhaled a small sigh of satisfaction. It was enough to draw the attention of his companion.

'You awake too?'

Slowly his great body turned towards her.

'We should be getting up soon,' he whispered.

She reached for him. It was some time before they surfaced again. Disentangling himself from her arms, Carson cautiously parted the makeshift curtain and peered into the living quarters.

A fire crackled in the large fireplace. There was a stillness about the gloomy room and he realized the cabin must be empty except for him and Sandra. He grinned and looked down at the woman curled up beneath the coverings. Like a cat, he thought.

Her eyes, smoky with love, held his for a few moments.

'It looks as if we are alone,' he told her as he stretched mightily and then reached for his clothes.

Her eyes were on his magnificent body as he yawned. Her admiration was evident as she observed the movement of the muscles as they rippled under his pale skin. She placed her hand on the small of his back in a purely affectionate gesture. Very quickly he pulled on his shirt and reached for his breeches.

'I wonder what the time is?'

She shrugged in answer. It was her turn to yawn. He stamped into his boots and quickly pulled on the rest of his garments.

Going over to the fireplace he peered into a large black pot suspended on a hinged iron bar that could be swung to dangle over the fire. Within the pot was a generous quantity of corn meal. From a shelf he took earthenware bowls and ladled out two copious helpings.

He was not sure if he should be helping himself but he was too hungry to care. In the act of spooning the meal into the bowls his stomach grumbled as the smell of the cooked grains drifted up from the pot. When he turned back to the room Sandra joined him from the sleeping quarters.

They sat at the rough table and ate. Sandra watched fascinated as she observed her companion. Three bowls later he walked over to the fire for another helping. The door opened and the elderly lady who had tended to their needs last night entered. Carson stood looking guiltily from the almost empty pot to the woman.

'I . . . I think I . . . I . . .'

'Good morning,' she greeted him. 'I trust you slept well.'

The old woman looked into the almost empty pot and smiled her toothless smile.

'I'll get you some bread.'

She slapped two plates on the table followed by a large loaf and a knife. Carson hacked away at the bread and pushed large hunks smothered in butter into his mouth. The old woman poured them both pitchers of milk.

'It's time to find out what's going on,' he said, at last getting up from the table.

His hostess fluttered round him smiling up at his great height and girth.

'You will be back for dinner, master.'

He grinned back down at her.

'Why, what's for dinner, corn meal?'

She giggled, her toothless mouth gaping as she watched him get ready to go outside.

He picked up the axe that had done such bloody work the previous day. His revolver was already in his holster. It had nestled beneath his pillow during the night. His hosts had not insisted on disarming him within their village, which was slightly surprising. He surmised that because of his valiant efforts during the battle at the ranch they regarded him now as an ally.

He glanced at Sandra with an enquiring look on his face. She smiled back at him.

'I'll follow you shortly. There's certain thing's a girl's got to see to.'

The feeling of well being lasted about ten paces from the front door. As he eyed the lazy smoke rising from chimneys the sudden thump of racing hoofs reverberated towards him. Carson stopped dead and stared ahead. He could see the riders coming down the street.

As he dropped to a fighting crouch he snatched his revolver from his belt. Just as he was turning he saw a rider bearing down on him. The man tossed a bundle over Carson's head even as he fired at the rider. As the ranger's bullet knocked the man from his horse there was a deafening explosion behind him and something heavy crashed on top of him flinging him forward into the street.

26

He was fleeing from his hometown of Perdue. There had been no time to prepare for his flight — no suitable clothes or even food. He had been running from the brutal gangs controlled by General Rodriguez. He had also been running from the dreadful image of his grandfather swinging on a rope — hung there on the whim of the bandits in the service of General Rodriguez.

That first week was hard. Used to the cheering heat of the forge he had been plunged into the comfortless life of a vagabond. He had wandered through the countryside hungry and distressed. Only his strong constitution kept him going. Towards the end of the week a wagon train had picked him up. They rescued the starveling from his wandering life and he travelled with them to the nearest settlement.

That had been the beginning of a new life. He had become a recruit in the Texas Rangers, where his strength, youth and determination to succeed had brought acclaim from his commanders. Scarce a few months later he was a fully-fledged ranger, skilled in the use of the new Colts just becoming available to the rangers. His home was now Company E of the Texas Rangers.

With a rush he remembered where he was — remembered the oncoming rider and the sticks of dynamite curling over his head. As he became more aware of his surroundings he heard the continuing crackle of rifles and the deafening clump of dynamite exploding. It was evident from the noise the battle was ongoing.

He groaned and tried to move. For a moment panic tugged at him. He could see and feel and hear but he could not move. There was an almost overwhelming impulse to scream as he struggled against the beams pinning him against the ground. He began taking deep breaths to calm himself. When he was once again in control he began to take stock.

His arms were trapped beneath his body. There was no way of exerting any pressure to free himself from the crushing weight on his upper back. He drew on his considerable stamina inflating his chest and hoping to gain a little space but nothing moved. It was as if he were trying to lift a house — the foundations of which had been built over his body.

He could feel the revolver in his hand where he had snatched it from the holster when he saw the raiders. But the weapon was trapped beneath his body along with his hands. He heaved again and felt the heaviness of the wreckage weighing him down.

As he lay helpless he sensed the attack on the stockade was petering out. The explosions had ceased while the rifle fire was becoming sporadic.

He listened — straining to make

sense of the noises around him. The firing had almost ceased. He could hear shouting as if someone was issuing orders. The voices drew nearer.

Someone not far from him was calling out for help. It was a woman's voice. With a sudden dread he wondered if it might be Sandra. Perhaps trapped, as he was himself, under the rubble of the wrecked cabin? Abruptly a burst of gunfire erupted almost above him. The crying ceased.

He wanted to call out but knew it was prudent to keep quiet for now. Even if he was trapped and helpless he had a feeling he would be calling out for his own execution.

How had they found the settlement? What had gone wrong? Surely Black Ben would have lookouts posted. How had the attackers broken through to the village?

He lay there with his thoughts in turmoil. His anxiety for Sandra was acute. He did not want to think the unthinkable. But he could not block out the knowledge that the debris pinning him down was the wreckage from the cabin where he had spent the night.

There were more shouted orders and gunshots. Carson reckoned they were laying waste to the village and finishing off any survivors.

Carson raged at his helplessness. He should be up there protecting the inhabitants of the settlement. His chest heaved as he took deep breaths and tried to lift, as if by willpower alone, the massive weight of whatever was holding him. But he was held in a rigid confinement with despair biting into him, sapping his strength and energy.

As he struggled with his frustration and rage he became aware of the stillness from above. He stopped struggling and remained quiet as he strained to determine what was happening in the village. Nothing!

Where children had played and dogs barked — where the inhabitants had gone about their normal life, now there came an ominous silence. It was the second time in his young life that he felt such impotence.

The first had been the occasion of his grandfather's murder when he had been unable to help the old man that had meant so much to him. He pushed his face hard into the dusty street and gave himself up to despair.

He may have dozed off or passed out — he could not be sure. Some noise had awoken him. He strained to listen. His body was numb. He felt as if his body had become part of the earth. It was with great difficulty he managed to move his head. He could move nothing else. Whatever it was that had fallen on him held him securely. Even if it meant a hail of bullets he knew he had to call for help. He could not survive much longer beneath the crushing weight on his body.

'Help.'

His voice was a low croak. He tried again and this time a stronger sound emerged.

'Down here! Under here! Help! Help!'

There was an excited babble of voices. Then scrabbling noises above him.

'Hang on, we can see you.'

He let his head drop forward and awaited his fate.

'Over here, we've found someone.'

Carson let himself go — fading in and out of consciousness. At last hands were tugging at him. He tried to assist his rescuers but his muscles, so long cramped in the one position, would not respond.

'Christ, it's Carson! Get him to the fire.'

He felt hands grabbing for him and then he was dragged from his tomb. A huge fire, built with timbers from the ruined shacks, was sending out comforting waves of heat. Carson was placed near the blaze. A mug was pushed into his hand.

'Drink this.'

'Sandra,' he croaked, 'what happened to Sandra?'

Black Ben sat down beside him. He

was cradling a rifle in his arms and staring into the flames. Beyond him another figure squatted close to the fire. Carson stared around him. About a dozen people were crowding up to the fire — just staring into the flames. A large beam collapsed into the blazing centre sending up sparks and orange coloured flames. Black Ben made no response to his query.

27

Carson shivered violently. He raised the mug to his lips and half-drained the contents. The fiery spirits went down quickly and he began to cough. A warm glow began somewhere deep inside and he could feel life beginning to return to his paralysed body. When he got his breath again he looked towards the man beside him.

'Sandra . . . the others . . . what about them?'

The black-bearded man turned his head and looked full at the young ranger. Carson saw the anguish in his face. He stared back, suddenly full of apprehension.

'What is it?' he whispered with fear like broken glass twisting inside. 'What is it?'

Black Ben shook his head.

'The whole village . . . '

As if lost for words Black Ben abruptly stood up and slowly looked around him like a man who has lost his way. Shivering with apprehension, Carson stood up and also looked around him. He blinked in disbelief then shook his head.

'No,' he whispered.

When their little party arrived last night they had entered a thriving settlement. Rows of log cabins had nestled in the narrow valley. Men, women and children had come out to greet the returning fighters. They had jostled with each other to call out greetings to their men folk. Now he found himself looking round at the smouldering remains of a scene from hell.

Smoke-blackened ruins were all that marked the dwelling places that had looked so picturesque last night. Where chimneys had sent hazy smoke up into the clear skies now the stone flues jutted stark and lifeless like accusing fingers pointing to the heavens.

Carson felt the bile rise within him. For the first time he turned to take note of the people who were gathered round Black Ben. With some relief he saw Henrietta. Middett was there along with fighters he recognized from the battle at the ranch. The twins Lisa and Tessie were there.

'This is everyone?'

Black Ben nodded.

'A lot of us were out of the village this morning when the attack occurred. Some of us were taking the livestock to a safe place — we keep them separate from the stockade. We do this because if we were attacked we could still run and know the animals were safe. Your girls decided to come with us. They left you sleeping.'

Carson turned blindly and began stumbling back to the spot where he had been trapped. Black Ben put out a hand as if to stop him, then let it drop. The survivors watched him come to a stop before the ruins. He stood swaying uncertainly while all the time staring at the wreckage.

The roof had collapsed trapping anyone inside. The dynamite must have landed as he had left, blowing out the roof and setting fire to the building. Some of the timbers had landed on him and pinned him to the ground. It was obvious no one inside could have survived the blast and subsequent fire.

Tears streamed down his face. He fell to his knees. There were footsteps behind him and he felt a hand on his shoulder. He turned his distraught face around and saw it was Henrietta. Suffering as he was, he was still able to see the tears in her eyes as she gazed down at him.

'I'm sorry, Carson . . . '

Gratefully he grabbed her delicate hand in his and held it there on his shoulder, glad of someone to comfort him in his anguish.

'Come,' she urged him, 'come back to the fire. When you've recovered we'll have to make plans.'

He rubbed fiercely at his eyes and

face and slowly stood.

'This is another debt Rodriguez owes me. I will avenge you, Sandra. I will avenge you.'

It was a subdued group that gathered by the bonfire trying to take some comfort from the lively flames flickering through the salvaged wood.

'How did they get in? I thought you had guards posted. You should have had warning of such a large force moving up on the village.'

Black Ben coughed harshly and spat into the flames. Some of his men were piling more wood onto the fire. There was no shortage of fuel from the ruined houses.

'Don't you think I've been trying to work that out. We were betrayed. We should have had plenty of warning. Our lookouts must have been taken by surprise. I've sent scouts to find out what has happened to them. They'll be back any time now.' He shook his head grimly. 'When I find out who it was . . .'

He stopped suddenly. A young woman dressed in furs was seen approaching. The group around the fire turned and watched her advance.

Carson could see she was very young — a few years younger than him — about fifteen at most. He had never seen her before but then that was not surprising considering the short time he had been among these people. Abruptly she stopped in front of Black Ben. He did not speak. Instead he pulled out a bottle and handed it to her. There was silence among the group of survivors as they watched her uncork the bottle and take a long swig. Wiping her mouth, she shuddered as she handed the bottle back.

She pulled back the hood covering her head and a cascade of golden hair spilled out. Her hair of golden braids was a surprising contrast to the dull colour of the furs she wore. The group around the bonfire seemed hypnotised as she shook her blonde tresses and then used her hands to draw the bright hair back from her face.

'They're all dead,' she stated simply.

The words hung in the air. Spoken quietly it had the power to shock Carson. His hands bunched by his side as if he was readying himself to attack though no obvious foe were near.

'Knifed where they stood guard.' She paused before continuing. 'There were no defence wounds.'

Carson interrupted her. 'What do you mean — no defence wounds?'

Her head turned to him. Eyes colder than ice pierced him to the brain.

'You were the one that slept in my mother's house last night?' Staring grimly at Carson she continued. 'It means that they knew and trusted the attacker — the traitor. He would have visited the outpost on some pretext and then when they least expected it he knifed them. This man was an ally — someone they trusted. It was so unexpected. They stood no chance. He must have then led Rodriguez's men into the settlement. We have no traitors in our midst. It must have been a newcomer.'

She was staring hard at Carson. He could sense the accusation in her voice.

'What are you suggesting?' he burst out. 'Are you saying it was one of us?'

28

She moved with the swiftness of a cat. Carson was unable to react in time. The knife was at his throat and her face was inclined up at him — a pale smudge in the twilight.

'The traitor was not one of us,' she hissed. 'You brought him here. Now my mother is dead. She was all the family I had.'

Carson stared into those icy blue eyes and recognized the killing rage in them. Her blade was held steady against his neck. He knew she was quite capable of pushing the knife into his throat. Helpless against her fury he did nothing — just stared back, still numbed by his own grief at losing Sandra in the holocaust.

'Katrina, enough!'

It was Black Ben who broke the spell. 'This man almost died in the attack.

We found him buried in the wreckage. He's a victim just as much as you. His own woman . . . ' the speaker hesitated as if afraid of causing Carson more pain, ' . . . she died in the house along with your mother.'

For long tense moments she stood there. Carson could feel the tension in her as she stared up at him, her eyes like a snake about to strike.

'I still believe it was one of your friends killed my mother,' she hissed at last. 'They brought the bandits into the town and slaughtered our people. I will kill him when I find him.'

With that she sheathed her knife inside her furs and turned her back on him. Carson felt the tension drain out of him only to be replaced by anger. Suddenly he raised his arms in the air and screamed into the oncoming night.

All the frustration he had felt as he lay trapped underneath the wreckage — all the grief over his loss was built into that cry. His anguished howls rang across the ruined houses and out into the dusty hills. Then it seemed a cloud of despair and despondency descended on the group gathered round the blazing bonfire and no one spoke for what seemed a very long time.

'Gather round everyone.'

Black Ben at last broke through the haze of apathy that seemed to have gripped the company.

'We must decide what to do.'

There was a stirring of shadows and a scraping of boots as people looked towards their leader.

'I think it would not be wise to stay here. We'll have to move to somewhere safer. It is possible they might return to finish us off once and for all. The question is where do we go? But whatever we do we've got to move out.'

He waved a hand around at the devastation.

'Find yourselves a place to sleep. I think we'll be all right here for tonight. But to be on the safe side we'll replace the lookouts. I could do with some volunteers to go out there and keep our dead comrades company.'

A stirring of activity broke out as men parcelled out the duties. Someone was taking charge. There was purpose to their lives once more. Where Black Ben led they would follow.

Carson stared speculatively at the trapper. He felt the glimmering of an idea was pushing to the front of his mind.

'You haven't any real plans, have you?' he questioned the man.

Black Ben shook his head.

'This has thrown out all our plans. We'll just have to take it a day at a time. Move out, find a new base and start over again.'

'Would you be prepared to join forces with others who are enemies of General Rodriguez?'

'What do you mean, laddie?'

Carson hesitated for a moment before answering.

'Did you know that Rodriguez intends to head down into Mexico. The plan is to join up with rebel forces and take over the government of Mexico.'

Black Ben slowly scratched his beard.

'So! That's good news for us. If Rodriguez goes south that means he'll not be around to harass us.'

'Yes, but if Rodriguez succeeds in setting himself up as ruler of Mexico he can send arms and men across the border to root out his enemies. They'll clear out these foothills and slaughter you like they would vermin.'

For a few moments the two men stared at each other. Carson's plan was to persuade Black Ben to join with him and help to deliver Henrietta to her father. Suddenly he was unsure if it was such a good idea to enlist the trapper. However for the moment he could think of nothing better, so he ploughed on.

'I was on my way south to deliver Henrietta to her father. If Rodriguez captures her he can use her to bargain with her father, maybe even force him to join him in his bid for power. If we can evade Rodriguez and deliver

Henrietta safely to her father we can join forces with him. Then we may get a chance to strike at Rodriguez before he makes his bid to take over. Think about it. On your own, it's only a matter of time before you're driven out. By coming with me you'll be placing yourself in alliance with a man who also wants Rodriguez brought down.'

The trapper looked speculatively at the speaker. His bearded face gave nothing away.

'I did wonder about you. Why, for instance, is Rodriguez so desperate to recapture you? True enough, you escaped from him. So he wants the girl to get a hold over her father.'

Carson nodded his head and stared into the bright flames leaping through the timbers that had been salvaged from some of the wrecked dwellings.

He was still reeling from the impact of the suspicion that Katrina had cast on him and his small band. His own sense of loyalty could hardly visualize such a betrayal. He was convinced it had to be one of the trappers that had betrayed them. None of the people he had brought here would be capable of such duplicity. He would have to be wary of everyone now. The safety of Henrietta was paramount and he could not imperil her any more than was necessary.

'I have to make the journey south to deliver the girl to her father. I can tell you he will be grateful to you for your help and will make you welcome. By helping me do this thing you will strike a blow against Rodriguez. In all probability you will also have the opportunity of fighting against him.'

Black Ben stared hard at his fellow refugee. In the short time he had known him he had formed a grudging respect for the youngster. He greatly admired the way the young ranger had handled himself during the battle at the women's ranch. Now he was asking him to uproot himself from the hills in which he had hunted and trapped for a goodly part of his life. Ruefully he realized his options were limited.

'Life has not been easy for us. Now that this stockade has been destroyed it will mean even more hardship. We will have to establish another place. There are settlements scattered about that would give some help. But their assistance, by necessity, would be meagre for their own resources are slender.'

Black Ben hawked and spat into the fire.

'My people are demoralized by the loss of their loved ones and friends.'

He sighed deeply and fell silent.

Carson kept quiet. He sympathized with Black Ben. His own loss had almost deadened him to the necessity for any coherent action. Only the thought of his duty to the rangers and the necessity of delivering Henrietta to the safety of her home were driving him on to make plans.

'A leader almost always has hard choices to make,' his companion continued eventually. 'Each time we set out on a hunting trip I did so with the knowledge that some of my men might never return. If it weren't Indians attacking it were bandits. I've had to live with the effects of that — the grieving family and friends — the gaps in the ranks that have to be filled. I ask myself, how much more can my people take?'

He stared hard at his companion.

'I'm gonna ask my little band to make up their own minds. You speak first and tell them what you've told me. Then I'll explain the options to them. After that I'll let them vote.'

Carson nodded.

'It's only fair.'

He looked at the motley band huddled around the blazing bonfire. Henrietta was staring over at him as if she knew he was engaged in the process of deciding their fate. He closed his eyes and unbidden the vision of Sandra floated before him.

It seemed to him that the people he loved were being plucked from him one by one by the hand of a cruel fate. For a moment he wavered in his resolution to carry on in his endeavours to protect Henrietta.

He knew that if he failed in this one task he would be seeking death. The death would be not by his own hand but by the hand of the enemy for he would hurl himself at the people who were the cause of his loss and grief and hope to kill as many as possible before he perished. But in that moment of weakness he knew he could not take that contrived way out of his responsibilities. He could only seek refuge in death when the one man he held responsible for his woes accompanied him on that one-way journey.

Sadness weighed heavily on him. He sat staring into the fire feeling tired and dispirited. Then sleep — sleep that was supposed to heal and rest the mind — settled on him and his dreams were filled with night terrors.

29

Slowly he opened his eyes. The great fire that had burned the night before was a heap of dulled ashes. Reluctantly he sat up and discovered someone had draped a blanket over him while he had slept. He could hear people moving about and voices.

'Libby, it's Libby.'

She came riding in slumped across her horse. The twins crowded round her as she wearily slid to the ground. Carson watched as the young girls escorted her across to the fire. There was blood on her face. She saw him watching and stopped — tried to smile. He could not speak. She was a painful reminder of what he had lost — the companion of his dead lover.

Black Ben came up and the remnants of his tribe gathered round. Someone had been brewing coffee. They handed a mug to the woman. Gratefully she sipped — the steam from the hot drink drifting up across her blood-streaked face. She stared at Carson through the vapour.

'Diego,' she said at last.

Her head turned and she scanned the crowd.

'Where's Sandra?'

The twins by her side started weeping. In spite of her own hurts the big woman gathered the girls to her. They buried their faces in her bulk and sobbed. Her eyes were on Carson. There were dark circles underneath. His pain was reflected in her own expression.

'What about Diego?'

It was Black Ben who asked the question. Her eyes were still on Carson as she replied.

'He betrayed us.' She took a deep, shuddering breath before continuing. 'We were together. In the night he left. I followed. He was saddling his horse. When he discovered me he asked me to go with him. He was starting a new life away from all this. Like a fool I believed him. Once away from the settlement he did this to me.'

She indicated the blood on her face.

'While I was helpless he tied me up. This morning he came and released me. Then he rode away. If I'd had a gun I would have shot him. But then . . . I am just a fat, foolish woman . . . '

She dropped her head then and held the twins, united in their sorrow.

'We will go with you, Carson,' Black Ben said. 'Perhaps it is right to take the fight to General Rodriguez.'

The livestock were gathered and brought to the settlement. The wisdom of keeping the animals separate from the stockade was now evident as they shared out the horses. There were more than enough mounts for the survivors. With what pathetic belongings could be salvaged from the ruins, they set out.

It was a despondent crowd of migrants that rode away from the ruined settlement — uncertain of what the future held for them.

Ahead of them, Katrina, the fierce and lovely girl who had lost the last member of her family in the raid, scouted for danger. When they camped that night she came into the fire and made her report.

'Somebody is watching us,' she said as she ate. 'The danger is when we have to come down out of these hills. The passes are narrow and ideal for ambush.'

'Who? Is it Rodriguez?'

'I don't know. They don't show themselves. It's as if they're waiting to get us to where they want us before attacking.'

'You think it'll be these passes we have to traverse?'

The lovely blond hair was tied back with a piece of rawhide. This girl allowed nothing to emphasize her gender. She was a scout first and foremost. Her womanhood was naught against the job she had to do.

'What if we sent a small group to

draw them out?'

It was Carson's contribution after listening to Black Ben and Katrina.

Black Ben nodded.

'Who would lead such an outfit?'

'I'll take them,' Carson offered, 'half a dozen or so to probe the passes and find a safe passage through. Then we can report back to the main party. If all is well we hurry everybody through.'

'Good enough — leave at first light.'

Henrietta approached him when she learned of his mission. Since Libby had returned with the news of Diego's treachery the girls had bonded into a little group. Even Katrina was part of the cluster.

'I hear you are to scout ahead,' she said.

He nodded, busy with saddling up his mount.

'You will take care?'

Surprised, he turned and stared at her. She dropped her eyes as if embarrassed by this show of concern.

'I mean, we keep losing people,' she

muttered. 'I . . . I . . . don't want to lose any more . . . friends.'

Her words were hesitant as if she was forcing herself to speak them. She raised her hand in a diffident gesture then dropped her arm and walked away.

He stared after her, not knowing what to make of her behaviour. Then he shrugged and swung onto his horse and led his little band out of the encampment.

They were well up the pass before anything happened.

When the shot came it took everyone by surprise.

Carson had leaned forward to adjust his stirrup. He felt he was riding with one leg higher than the other. Behind him a man was plucked from the saddle as the bullet punched him in the chest. The horse whinnied shrilly and reared in the air.

Carson was sure he felt the closeness of the next bullet as it passed over his head. It hit the plunging horse in the neck. The horse staggered and blood erupted from its mouth as it opened it to emit a shrill scream. Carson was swiftly off his own mount and rolling for cover at the side of the narrow trail that wound up the side of the pass.

A small boulder was the only protection he could find. He was scanning ahead as he tried to locate the ambushers. It was a hopeless task. The gunmen could be anywhere on the rocky walls.

Around him the trappers were scrambling from their horses as they, like him, sought some protection from the gunfire. Abandoned horses milled around and then took off back down the way they had come. One of the trappers leapt towards the horses and tried to stem the flight. A shot cracked out again. Carson heard the man curse but was too busy looking ahead to see what his fate was.

The faintest telltale smudge of smoke drifted up from a point on the rim of the pass. Carson locked on to this point, not daring to take his eyes from this location. Gently he eased his rifle forward. His front sight hovered just above the gunman's vantage point. He narrowed his eyes.

There would be only one opportunity to hit his man and the chance of success was not good. However, his shot or shots might be close enough to dislodge the gunman from the ridge.

Patiently he waited. Behind him the survivors of the ambush tried to make themselves as small as possible.

30

'Can anyone see them?'

'I think I have spotted one of them, I'm waiting for him to try another shot and show himself,' Carson answered — his attention never wavering from the rockface. 'Who's hurt?'

'Simon's dead. Drilled through the chest. His horse was wounded but it galloped back with the others when they panicked. Gordon took one in the arm. We can't help him while that bushwhacker's got us pinned down like this.'

'Don't worry about me. Just put one in his head for me. This arm hurts like the devil.'

The tension mounted as the little group watched the rim from where the shots had come. The gunmen or gunman could keep them pinned down for as long as they chose. All he had to do was fire an occasional shot towards them. They would be obliged to keep their heads down. Carson cursed the delay.

So intense was his gaze his eyes began to smart. He wanted nothing more than to put down his rifle and rub his irritated eyes. Another shot rang out. Something ricocheted from a rock and spun down to kick up dirt from the path.

Carson saw the puff of smoke before he heard the report of the shot. He fired instinctively at the site of the feathery wisp of gun smoke, more to send a message to the marksman than with any hope of hitting anything.

He figured the gunman had fired blindly, just aiming in their general direction to keep them there. It could be that he was expecting reinforcements and planned to keep them pinned down until more men arrived.

Behind him Carson could hear the men cursing as they tried to burrow into the hard rock of the pass. He cursed some himself as he desperately tried to figure a way out of this predicament.

They had only ridden a few miles from the main body of survivors. Now they were stranded, their mounts scattered back down the trail and isolated from the remainder of the group. Carson felt the strands of frustration winding through him as he tried to calm his mind and work out a plan to extricate them from the situation.

After the last shot the silence seemed to deepen in the little gorge. When they had started only a short time ago the sky was dull and overcast — holding the promise of rain. Carson was not sure if rain would be a blessing or not. If heavy enough it might provide enough cover to go either forward or backward. The thought gave him an idea.

'Listen, you men,' he called out. 'I know roughly where that bushwhacker is located. If he knows his job he'll move about some. If we can harass him, he'll have to fire blindly or take a chance and show himself. I want two or three decent shooters to bang away at the last place I spotted his smoke. While you're doing that, I'll rush further up the pass and try and find a way to the top.'

Without turning round he raised his arm and pointed to the rim above.

'See that part of the rocks that bulges out slightly — then there's a lot of greenery just below it — well, that's roughly where the gunman is working. When I give the signal I want you men immediately behind me to lay down fire along that part of the rim. Spray your shots about twenty yards either side. Just keep firing intermittently so that when one man isn't firing his companion is. While you're keeping the bushwhacker busy, one of you go back down the pass and rescue the horses. I'll run up the pass and try to find a way to the top. And then we'll nail that booger if he's not either dead or fled.'

He waited a few moments before continuing.

'You all clear what you have to do?'

There were grunts from various members of his little force.

'Good. I'm going to wait a few minutes and then I'll raise my arm. On that signal everyone start firing. Then I'll stand up and start running.'

He waited while his eyes squinted through the sights of his rifle. The shot when it came almost made him jump. It was a good moment for him. He saw the puff of smoke and automatically fired. Without waiting for the signal of his raised arm his men poured a withering hail of firepower along the place he had shown them. The bush-whacker had moved but not too far and some of their shots must have come close to his position.

'Keep firing! Keep firing!'

Carson jumped to his feet and raced up the trail.

31

As he ran he concentrated on keeping from stumbling on the uneven ground. From time to time he glanced at the rock walls on either side, searching for some means of getting to the top.

He was angry now — angry with the bushwhacker for hindering their progress but also angry with himself for being in this predicament.

The noise of gunfire echoed around him, blocking out the pounding of his feet on the rock-strewn surface.

Doggedly he ran — making good progress but finding no way up either side of the pass. Just ahead was a jumble of large boulders created at sometime by a rock fall. It was with some relief that he flung himself into this rocky shelter.

His chest was heaving from his sprint up the trail and he was leaking sweat.

Gun in hand, he scanned the rocks above him.

Carson took stock of his position. Gunfire still echoed from the men he had left behind. He suddenly thought the men giving covering fire were now in the most vulnerable position. At least he now had decent cover. The man who had gone back to round up the horses would be out of danger but those left behind were still at risk from the gunman on top of the pass.

If the bushwhacker were joined by reinforcements then those men would be even more at risk. It was up to him to kill the gunman and do it soon before reinforcements arrived. It was then he saw the crack in the rock face and a glimmer of hope surfaced in this fraught situation.

At some stage there must have been a tremor in the earth and the rock wall had split apart. It would explain the boulders lying by the trail that now provided such excellent cover for him. He eyed the crack for some moments. Then he laid his rifle on the ground.

The climb would not be made any easier with the axe strapped to his back but he did not fancy arriving on the top with only his revolver. Keeping a wary eye on the top of the pass he moved to the foot of the fissure and started to climb.

After a while he realized the ascent was not going to be as bad as he had feared. The fault that had fractured the rock had created jagged edges and there was plenty of hand and footholds.

He was making steady progress when the firing from below started again. Knowing he had no way of influencing the action below and because by now he was near the top he kept on going. At least he hoped the gunfire would distract the ambusher so his arrival on the top would go unnoticed.

For a few moments he hung there in the crevice, taking in deep breaths. When he thought he was ready he reached over his shoulder, loosened the axe in its makeshift sling and then went up and over.

A powerful heave from muscular shoulders and he rolled sideways bringing up his pistol and stopped.

Anxiously he scanned the top of the rise he had just climbed. His pistol swivelled, following the movement of his eyes. Slowly he lowered his weapon and cautiously rose to his knees. Every muscle tensed in readiness for action, he stood upright.

His shoulders sagged with relief. He was completely alone on the top. Whoever had fired on them was gone. Satisfied that this was the case he turned his attention back to the defile he had just quitted.

The firing had ceased. Lying full length he stretched out and peered over the edge. At first he could not make out what was happening and then he swore long and luridly as he saw the bandits swarming through the pass. The shooting began again. Rock chips stung his face and bullets buzzed around him before he realized the shooters were aiming at him. Hurriedly he drew back.

'Damn! Damn! Damn!'

As he swore he banged his fist on the ground in frustration. It looked like General Rodriguez's forces had swept up on the trappers while he had been climbing. Now he was isolated helplessly on top of the pass. In all probability the bandits had also overwhelmed Black Ben and the women.

'Damn! Damn you, Rodriguez.'

Carson recalled the day he had rescued Henrietta. That encounter seemed years ago but he knew it was only a matter of weeks. Now all his efforts to protect his charge had come to naught. General Rodriguez would use the girl as a pawn in his power play. The stakes were high, with Henrietta's father drawn in as an unwilling ally of the brutal Rodriguez.

Control of Mexico was the prize for the winner of that game. Rodriguez seemed to hold all the aces. In his short life Carson had never felt so impotent as he lay there not knowing what to do next. He rolled on his back and stared up at the dark clouds drifting slowly across the sky. With a weary sigh he forced himself to climb to his feet and begin walking.

32

The small group of horsemen coming unexpectedly upon the lone walker gave him no chance of escape.

Carson looked at the steep slopes on each side of the road and decided he would be easy prey on those inclines if they started shooting. There were too many for him to fight so he stood still and awaited his fate.

The bandits were grinning with pleasure as they approached.

'Drop your weapons,' the leader ordered.

When he did as ordered two of the horsemen scrambled down and draped him across a horse and efficiently tied his hands beneath its belly.

Carson felt his hair being gripped. His head was tugged back so that his face was in line with the man who was giving orders. The florid face of the bandit was inches from that of Carson.

'You are the gringo scum that beat Gondor.'

He could smell last night's beer on the man's breath and tried not to flinch. The man tugged harder at the handful of hair. Carson felt the pain in his neck as his head was pulled much further out of its natural line. He arched his back in a vain attempt to ease the pressure on his spine. The bandit, seeing his discomfort jerked violently and Carson's head came up only a fraction but the agony was excruciating.

'*Bastardo,*' he spat out. 'If you let me down off this horse I'll beat you worse than I did Gondor.'

'Is that so, you gringo piece of shit.'

Carson wasn't sure which was worse — the bandit's foul breath or the agony in his neck and spine. The man's black and broken teeth were probably the source of the vile breath.

'Listen, dogbreath, when my men come along to meet me here you and your scum will be buzzard meat.'

The bandit's knee smashed into his face and he almost screamed as the agony lanced through him. Pain exploded in his neck and back. As waves of agony coursed through him he was sure his neck had been fractured. He didn't believe his head could be dragged up much further but his tormentor wrenched savagely on his hair and through pain-dazed eyes he could see the man's face sneering at him.

'Gringo pig should not lie to me.'

Carson did not reply. He could not. The angle of his head was such that his throat was now constricted. He was finding it hard enough to breathe and quite impossible to talk. There was no telling how much more torture he would have had to endure but some of the bandits in the group intervened.

'Sergio, shouldn't we take him back to camp. While we wait for General Rodriguez we can have some fun with him. Gondor was a good friend of mine. We could give this gringo much pain before the general kills him.'

For moments more Sergio held Carson in the excruciating grip before he let go.

'Gringo shit,' he muttered and then yelled, 'Mount up. We'll take the pig back with us.

★ ★ ★

Carson stared up at the man he had sworn to kill. He thought now of that fateful day that had launched him on an eventful and painful journey that had taken him to the company of rangers then on to eventual captivity.

His companion on that journey had been Henrietta and he had fought Rodriguez's champion, Gondor to win his freedom.

He had loved and lost on the way and the memory of that interlude in his life still hurt. Now the man who had pushed him into this eventful string of trials stood before him and Carson felt a little tingle of apprehension. This man had the power of life or death over him. If the bandit chief so wished, he was dead for sure. Dead before he had managed to fulfil his promise to rescue Henrietta and dead before he could wreak his revenge.

His back and neck and head ached abominably and every movement seemed to bring on excruciating agony.

General Rodriguez stood before him now and he looked as big as a buffalo bull and twice as formidable.

'I see my men have been entertaining you,' Rodriguez observed as he stared down at the battered man.

It was not easy to distinguish the features of the prisoner through the mask of dried blood and dirt. His nose and lips were swollen from the beating he had received at the hands of Sergio and his companions.

The bandits had taken it in turns to hit their helpless victim with thickly knotted ropes. As the beaters went about their brutal work they screamed abuse at their captive. The continual hitting with the crude bludgeons and the shouting reduced most men to quivering terror. But Carson was no ordinary mortal.

True, he had been subjected to a gruelling amount of violence in the last few weeks, which had taken its toll on even his great reserves of strength. But he had a stubborn, dogged streak that refused to be beaten into submission.

General Rodriguez had arrived back at the camp and when told of Carson's capture had come to see the man who had killed his champion and then escaped with the girl he hoped to use as a bargaining chip.

Before he could continue his examination of the prisoner a young woman burst through the door followed by a couple of bandits.

All heads turned to the doorway. Carson blinked in surprise. Henrietta confronted Rodriguez who looked faintly amused as he looked at the girl.

'How dare you keep me in captivity

like this, you animal?'

Henrietta's face was tight with rage as she ground out the words. In spite of his own little world of pain Carson could only stare in admiration at the girl. This was his first indication that she was safe. That was, if being in the power of Rodriguez could be called safe.

'Carson!'

Before anyone could intervene she had darted past the bandit chief and flung herself at the bloodied man tied to the post.

'What have they done to you?'

Carson winced as the girl wrapped her arms around him and squeezed his battered, hurting body. He tried to say something but his voice would not work.

Rodriguez was barking out orders and there was a flurry of movement within the room. Men were milling around the girl and hands were reaching out to pluck her away. He felt the sharp edge of something being pushed into his bound hands. Then the girl was being hauled away from him.

33

'Take your hands off me, you peons. I'm the daughter of Senor Xavier.'

She was magnificent. Her scornful voice lashed the bandits manhandling her. But these men were more fearful of their leader. While the struggle was going on Rodriguez moved to confront his prisoner. He took out a long cavalry sword and placed the tip under Carson's chin.

'Carson, I have a feeling you have caused me enough trouble.'

The bandit chief removed the tip of his sword from Carson's chin and pushed it into his nostril instead.

Carson stared back at Rodriguez as the painful pressure of the blade inside his nostril forced his head back. The bandit leader was frowning as he studied his captive.

'The heroic ranger on the day

Senorita Henrietta slipped from my grasp when I had successfully ambushed her escort.'

The pressure of the sword increased. Carson arched his head further under the pressure of the sharp edge.

'You almost broke my goddamned arm that day.'

Carson could do nothing as the steel blade bored deeper and deeper. The pain was excruciating. His nose had been broken during his brutal interrogation. He could not prevent the groan that now escaped him. Carson was not to know how near death he was. Yet the bandit chief hesitated to push the deadly blade all the way.

'Then you kill my champion. When I offered you my protection and hospitality, what did you do? You sneak around my camp in the night, kill my guards and steal my horses. Not only that, you forcibly remove my valued guest, Senorita Henrietta Xavier, from my protection. You are like a poison snake that I would stamp on. I could kill you now but I have other plans for your death.'

Slowly the general withdrew the blade from his helpless victim. He held the sword up and contemplated it for a few seconds.

'I have a magnificent Spanish pure-bred warhorse named Xolotl. He hungers for blood, does my faithful warhorse. He was bred for war. I have captured your friends and they are even now preparing to participate in an exciting sport for Xolotl and me. Would you like to join them?'

Abruptly the general sheathed his sword.

'Take him out to the field. Tell Gonzales to include this ape in the line-up.'

He turned and smiled at the girl now held firmly between two bandits.

'Time for a little sport, my dear. You seem a trifle over-wrought. It will do you good to watch your champion on the killing field. Just as long as he doesn't lose his head.'

General Rodriguez stalked from the room. As she was dragged after him Henrietta gave Carson one last despairing look. Preoccupied as he was with hiding the blade she had passed to him, he made no response. Then he too was being dragged outside.

With men on both sides and his arms bound, Carson could see no opportunity for escape. He had only the concealed blade Henrietta had slipped him. It was like an ace up his sleeve but with Rodriguez holding a royal flush that did not seem much of an advantage.

He was led outside almost staggering with fatigue. It felt as if every bone in his body had been forcibly disjointed and then rammed back into their sockets again.

Even though the beating had ceased he could still feel the impact of the knotted ropes thudding against his head and body. He knew his nose was broken and guessed other bones were fractured. The mere effort of walking out to whatever fate the bandits had devised for him caused pain in every part of his battered body.

General Rodriguez's men had been busy. At regular intervals stout poles had been hammered into the rocky earth. As Carson was hustled along he saw men tied to these poles. His escort punched and kicked him as they forced him forward. He tried not to cry out as the blows landed on flesh already bruised beyond endurance.

The first man he recognized was Middett. The trapper looked as bloody as he was himself. There were other familiar figures tied to the poles. There was no sign of Black Ben.

Rodriguez's men were knocking an extra pole into the rocky soil. The posts were fashioned from young tree trunks sharpened at one end to make it easier to drive into the earth.

Carson was jostled towards this new stake and quickly roped in position. Hastily the field emptied leaving the row of trussed captives to guess at their fate.

Working at the blade passed to him by Henrietta, Carson managed to position it between his wrists. Surreptitiously he began to saw. As he worked he stared curiously about him.

The line up of trussed men suggested they were to be executed. He looked around for the firing squad. There was flickering movement overhead and he tried to stretch his much-abused neck upwards.

Vultures — those ancient harbingers of death. The dark shapes soared above the tethered men as if sensing the bloodletting that was to come.

His head drooped again as the ache in his spine intensified. He sagged against his post and felt it give slightly. Was the terrible pain in his body causing him to imagine things?

He tensed his legs and then let his weight drop forward. The ropes binding him dug cruelly into his arms but the rough post tipped with him. It was only slight but it was definite movement. He tensed and sagged as if struggling against his bonds. Anyone watching would see a man apparently striving to free himself from the ropes tethering him to the post. He hoped they would not suspect that his real objective was to dislodge the post itself.

There was a flurry of movement at the top of the field. He could see a huge Spanish stallion being saddled. This must be Xolotl, the horse Rodriguez had mentioned.

As he watched the activity he never stopped sawing at the ropes with his hidden blade. At the same time he kept pushing backwards and forwards in an attempt to slacken off the post.

He recognized the bulky figure of General Rodriguez. The bandit chief mounted the horse and the pair now cantered to the top of the field.

Carson watched as the man drew out the cavalry sword. He brandished the weapon about his head for a few practice swings then urged the horse towards the row of trussed-up figures. The bandit rode with the sabre resting on his shoulder. Suddenly Carson guessed what fate awaited the prisoners.

Horse and rider reached the first post. Carson tensed as he anticipated the stroke from the long blade. It did not come. Instead the bandit leader rode on down the line. As he got to Carson he reined in. Without warning he brought the sword down in a sweeping arc. Carson tried to wrench himself away from the trajectory of the blade but his bonds held him fast. The sword crashed down. The force of the blow drove his head down. Lights blazed inside his skull. There was a ringing in his ears.

34

Intolerable agony lanced through his body. He sagged limply against the post. If he hadn't been fastened with ropes he would be on the ground by now. He could hear Rodriguez's voice speaking to him.

'That's for causing me all this trouble. The next stroke will be with the edge of the blade.'

Carson stared dazedly at the ground. He could not raise his head. There was just too much pain. At last it registered that he had not received a deathblow. Rodriguez had used the flat of the blade to strike him.

Fighting the surging agony in his head he managed to raise his eyes towards the figure towering over him.

'You cringing coward,' he croaked, 'good at fighting helpless prisoners. Untie me and give me a blade. I'll ram it up your ass so hard you'll never ride a horse again.'

Rodriguez laughed out loud.

'Oh, I do admire a man with spirit.'

He whirled the blade around his head and made another swipe at the bound man. Carson felt the fresh agony as the blade sliced across his shoulder. Blood leaked through his shirt. Trying to ignore this new pain Carson glared defiantly at his tormentor.

'Go to hell, you bastard!'

Without further comment the general whirled his mount and cantered back along the line of prisoners. When he reached the top of the field he wheeled the great horse in a tight circle and with a yell set it running back down the line.

Carson sawed desperately at the rope. At the same time he rocked the post. Horse and rider were coming at a dead run now. Rodriguez reached the first prisoner, feinted with his blade and passed him by. He flashed by the second man and then with a sudden

261

twist of movement the blade lanced down and took the third prisoner in the neck.

The horse swept past and the man's head was lolling awkwardly to one side. Blood splashed onto his buckskin jacket and the body sagged lifelessly, held upright against the post by the ropes.

There was a mighty cheer from the assembled bandits. They were throwing their hats in the air and shouting encouragement to their general.

Horse and rider continued down the line. Again the bandit chief wheeled and cantered back to the top of the field. As he passed his victim he glanced curiously at the bloody corpse nodding as if in approval at his handiwork.

At the top of his run he turned and prepared to make the pass again. His men were still cheering on their leader. Rodriguez acknowledged his subordinates with a flourish of his blooded blade. The cheering grew wilder.

'Viva General Rodriguez!'

With a suddenness that surprised Carson the rope slackened as the blade finally cut through. Ignoring the pain in his tortured body, Carson gripped the post with his hands behind his back as if still tethered and began to rock frantically at the stake.

The wobble was very obvious now. He did not look up when he heard the thunder of the hoofs as Rodriquez started his run. The horse was reaching a gallop and rapidly approaching the line of prisoners once again. In sudden desperation Carson decided to risk everything. He pushed himself away from the post and swinging round grasped the rough tree trunk.

Behind him he could hear the heavy pounding of hoofs. There was a shout and guessed it came from the approaching horseman. He knew the bandit chief would have to ignore the other prisoners now. Carson, freed from his stake, would have to be dealt with.

This time the general wouldn't toy with him. That heavy blade would slice into his neck and decapitate him. Desperately he wrenched at the stubborn pole — so loose and yet adhering obstinately to its earthy crater.

The sound of pounding hoofs grew louder and louder. Not daring to look over his shoulder he heaved forward against the post then flung himself backwards. The upright pole held and he knew he had lost.

Rodriguez's heavy sword would not miss. Carson had witnessed the accuracy with which he had wielded the great sword as he beheaded his first victim.

Gathering his last shred of energy he threw his body forward. He had nothing to lose. A shadow fell over him and he tensed for the strike. Then he was falling forward as the post gave way. He felt the hair on the top of his head lift as something hissed over him. Then he was on the ground with the rough stake underneath him.

Hoofs pounded the ground close to him and he felt clods of earth patter down onto his body. For moments he lay there unable to move — not knowing what to do next. He knew he must get up and do something — soon very soon.

Someone was yelling his name.

'Carson! Carson! For Christ's sake, Carson, he's coming back.'

He recognized Middett's voice.

'Move, Carson, move. Shift your goddamn ass!'

His body was ripe agony. There was a pounding in his head. That drumming was bothering him. He knew he should do something about it.

'Carson!' Middett was yelling again.

From some reserve he found the energy to stand. His hands were still gripping the post and he used it to support him. That pounding — it still bothered him. Then he realized what it was. The hoof beats were coming back towards him.

The horse looked gigantic — huge muscled forelegs stretching and contracting as it carried the rider towards him. That was the drumming — it wasn't in his head — it was the sound of General Rodriguez galloping towards him on that huge horse.

Carson felt the rough bark of the young tree he now grasped in his hands. In the next few moments he was going to die. He stood one chance and one chance only. It had to work or he was dead.

Suddenly he screamed. It was not a scream of fear. It was a cry the warrior in him loosed.

Carson the fighter was not going down without a struggle. The killer instinct sent the adrenaline surging through his body. Tiredness, pain and fear were of no consequence — now was survival — now was life and death. Carson the warrior was still alive and ready to fight for survival.

Horse and rider thundered closer. Someone was screaming out his name. He ignored the shouting and concentrated on the task in hand.

The general and his devilish mount

were almost upon him. He felt the rough bark of the tree trunk and it sent a surge of power into him. The post felt big and powerful in his hands.

35

The sword was poised for a slashing movement that only had to hit home once and he was dead or disabled. Ignoring the bright blade he dropped onto one knee.

Everything happened very fast then. The sword arced towards him. Carson thrust the post low and hard. It went in between the forelegs of the galloping horse and was brutally whipped from his hands. At the same time Carson threw himself backwards. He almost made it but not quite. White-hot agony seared his head as the tip of the sword gouged a bright red line across his temple.

The wind was knocked out of his body as he crashed to the ground. He floundered on his back, struggling to get some air into his lungs. His head was a pulsating red and white agony. Somewhere a horse was screaming in torment. With a tremendous effort he managed to roll onto his front. Hands on the dusty earth — pushing hard — trying to stand. Shakily he was somehow on his feet.

He saw the horse then. It was thrashing about on the ground trying to push itself erect. There was something wrong with its forelegs. It was not getting them to work properly. The screaming stopped to be replaced by a piteous whinnying.

A great sadness swept over him. He had worked with horses most of his life. They were brought from the ranches and farms in the locality to be shod at the forge. It caused him great sorrow to see a beast in such distress. More so as he himself had caused the injury that brought it down.

He stumbled forward, arms out-stretched as if he would lift the crippled horse from the ground and set it on its feet again. Dropping to his knees beside the horse's head he was murmuring soothing words.

'Good boy, good boy.'

In response the great horse swivelled its neck and gripped his shoulder between powerful jaws. Carson felt the flesh tear as the powerful jaws bit deep. He gasped and tried to pull away. But the shoulder was held fast in a deathlike grip.

As he struggled in the paralysing clutch he saw beyond the horse a figure kneeling on the ground. The bulky shape of Rodriguez was scrabbling around searching for his fallen sword.

Carson's arm was growing numb under the bone-crunching jaws. In desperation he bunched his fist and punched the horse in the ear. The animal tried to pull away but still held on to the shoulder. With the agony in his arm growing Carson frantically punched and punched again.

He saw Rodriguez stand. The general turned and faced Carson. In his hand he once more held his great sword.

'You gringo *bastardo!* You've ruined my goddamned horse — my beautiful

Xolotl. I'm going to slice you up bit by bit.'

Grimly he began to stalk forward.

Carson punched desperately at the horse. The arm in the animal's jaws was without feeling now. At last, the horse, unable to take that terrible pounding on its ear, released its hold. Carson cried out as the agony in his arm intensified. Through the pain he saw the huge figure of Rodriguez looming over him the sword held high.

'I'm gonna chop bits off till you beg me to finish you.'

Carson saw the chain. It lay across the saddle of the broken horse. With his good hand he wrenched at it. The sword had been aimed at his hand and struck sparks from the chain. Carson brought out his blade and slashed the rawhide holding the chain. As it came free Carson rolled away from the injured horse and its sabre-wielding rider. The sword was rising for another slash.

Desperately Carson swung the chain.

Sword and chain clanged together. The chain wound itself around the bright blade. By now Carson had his feet against the great bulk of the struggling horse. One-handed he heaved back on the chain. Taken by surprise Rodriguez tried to keep his balance but was dragged onto the horse. He stumbled, pitched headlong over his horse and plunged on top of his enemy.

Carson saw the general topple towards him. He tried to move out of the way but he was too tired — too hurt. The heavy body landed on top of him and punched the breath from his lungs. But Carson was still fighting for his life. Almost as the bandit crashed down Carson drove his forehead into the bandit's face.

Rodriguez grunted as the youngster's head crashed painfully into his nose. He retaliated by driving his knee up into Carson's groin. The new agony was just another pain in the youngster's much-abused body. Carson head-butted again and Rodriguez rolled away from him.

The bandit had held onto his sword and now with no room to swing the blade he smashed the handle into the side of Carson's head. Fresh agony seared through Carson as the blow landed on the sword wound inflicted earlier. He tried to twist away from his attacker. As he moved, the horse's head came round and it snapped at him. Fortunately for Carson the vicious teeth pinched inches short.

He could not but admire the fighting spirit of the injured beast. It was his actions that had damaged this magnificent horse. But he had no time for regrets.

Rodriguez had freed his sword from the entangling chain and was preparing to skewer his opponent.

36

Carson had only one good arm to fight with. The shoulder chewed by Xolotl had left that arm almost paralysed with harsh grinding pain every time he moved or had it jarred by his opponent.

With a supreme effort Carson managed to fend off the thrust that was aimed at his stomach. Desperately he swung the chain in a tight arc to form some sort of defense against the bandit's attack. Slowly he was being forced back.

Just keeping out of range of the slavering Xolotl he edged around the crippled beast. If he had been in full strength and uninjured perhaps he could have put his improvised weapon to better use. Now he could only swing the chain in defensive arcs and keep out of range of that deadly blade.

As they battled, shouts were echoing

from the top of the field and Carson suddenly remembered the followers of Rodriguez. His men would be rushing to the rescue of their leader. He almost despaired then. A fusillade of shots rang out and Carson could hear horses pounding down the field. At any moment those shots would find the range and blast him down. Just then an unlikely ally came to his aid.

Xolotl, the warhorse he had brought down, saw the feet come within range. The horse, maddened by pain and helplessness, fastened those wicked teeth into the calf just within its reach. That the calf belonged to its master was of no consequence. It was something on which it could take out its rage and pain and frustration. Rodriguez cursed and lashed out at the horse with his sword. For that fateful moment his guard was down.

Carson swung his improvised flail. He had to be quick. In all probability this would be his only chance to land a disabling strike. One-handed he started the trajectory of his weapon.

The chain was made of cast iron and weighed heavy. It was the only weapon Carson had to end the unequal fight.

Rodriguez sensed Carson's movement. Momentarily distracted by the savage attack of his beloved Xolotl his guard had slipped. Looking up he saw the chain swinging towards him. He tried to bring up his sword to block the clumsy weapon. He was a fraction late.

The chain slashed into the bandit's neck and wound around the throat. Carson pulled hard on the chain. The heavy links tightened around the general's neck. The bandit chief crumpled beneath the vicious blow.

With his larynx crushed, his mouth gaped wide as he tried to suck in air through his ruined gullet. His eyes widened and he clawed feebly at the brutal garrotte. His legs gave way and he tumbled across his beloved mount. He kicked and twitched as his lungs tried to drag in breath through his ruined throat. Carson kept up the pressure on the chain as he watched his enemy strangling.

'This is for you, grandad,' he gritted out as he watched the death throes of his garrotted enemy.

That faithful horse, Xolotl, instrumental in his master's downfall and feeling the familiar weight upon its back, tried pathetically to rise and carry its master once more.

Beside the labouring horse, threshing about in futile efforts to arise, Carson collapsed also. His legs suddenly gave way and he tumbled to the ground.

He sprawled helplessly beside the horse and its mortally wounded rider. Around him the earth vibrated. A forest of hoofs surrounded him. He listened to the violent shouts and sank deep into weary resignation and awaited the inevitable shots that would end his suffering.

The shot exploded right beside him. He jerked as the blast deafened him. There was no pain — at least no new pain. His whole body was one vast ache.

Slowly he allowed his attention to explore his hurting frame. He was convinced he had been shot but could not figure out where. Perhaps he still stood a chance. He kept a grip on the chain. That chain had served him well. Maybe he could take out a few more before he was killed outright.

Hands were lifting him. He swung the flail but his strength had gone. Poured out in that last bout with his enemy. The chain was raised an inch or two and his arm fell back.

'Damnit, the booger still wants to fight.'

Carson looked at the man who spoke.

Middett! Middett, who had been fastened to a stake awaiting the execution, was now kneeling beside him. His brain could not figure it all out. He was too tired — too much in agony. At least he had put paid to Rodriguez. He could rest in peace.

'Carson, you great big lummox, did you have to destroy Xolotl?'

It was Henrietta's voice.

With great effort he turned his head. Henrietta was staring down at him. There were tears in her eyes. Carson tried to speak. A dry croak emerged. The girl gestured behind her.

'It was my father's horse. Rodriguez stole him. Now both he and Xolotl are dead. Middett just put it out of its misery.'

Then she knelt beside him and squeezed his hand.

'Hang on in there,' her voice softened as she spoke. 'Don't worry. I'll take good care of you. It's my turn to look after you.'

Carson knew then he had died. Henrietta was being nice to him. He closed his eyes and sank into a dark and bottomless void.

37

They carried the unconscious ranger to the temporary camp. He was unaware of the great bustle of activity. Senor Xavier's personal physician attended to his numerous injuries. He worked for a couple of hours on the unconscious man. A worried Henrietta hovered around the surgeon, anxious to help.

Finally the medic finished and began to tidy away his instruments.

'How is he, doctor? Will he be all right?'

The physician, a narrow-faced man with a pencil thin moustache and with his slightly greying hair swept straight back from a prominent forehead, was washing his hands in a bowl. The water was stained pink with blood. He shook droplets of moisture from his hands and looked round for a towel before replying. Henrietta handed him a cotton cloth for him to wipe his hands. She frowned anxiously as she watched the doctor and waited for his verdict.

'He has cuts and abrasions all over his body. His head has been severely pummelled. His nose is broken along with his collarbone and maybe some bones in his face. He has lost a lot of blood and is suffering from severe exhaustion. I have done the best I can but his injuries, though not grave individually, could be life threatening if infection sets in. He must be kept in quiet seclusion.'

He looked at the young woman hanging avidly onto his every word. Suddenly he smiled.

'Senorita Henrietta, does this man mean something special to you?'

Henrietta stared at the doctor, unsure of what he meant. Before she could reply a tall, aristocratic man dressed in dark jacket and embroidered waistcoat entered the tent. The physician bowed courteously to the newcomer.

'Senor Xavier, I have done my best

for the patient, Senor Carson. He rests now which I think is his best hope. Plenty of rest and good food is what he needs now.' He shrugged. 'Nature must take its course. But he has in his favour a strong constitution and he has youth — both great aids in good recovery.'

'Oh, Father, perhaps when he is fit to be moved we can take him back home to recover?'

Senor Xavier moved to look down at the youth lying on the camp bed. He took note of the breadth of shoulders and deep chest of the young ranger. The patient's breathing was shallow and his skin had an unhealthy pallor.

'But he is so young! How could this youngster defeat the great General Rodriguez?'

He shook his head in puzzlement.

'Truly these Texans are a warrior race.'

'It was he who really defeated the bandits, Father.'

Henrietta had moved up beside her father.

'When they saw their leader fall they lost all heart. When Black Ben led you into their camp and you attacked them they broke and ran. Without Rodriguez to inspire them they were just a rabble.'

She reached out and laid her slim hand on Carson's forehead. Then she took a cloth and dampened it in the basin and wiped gently at the unconscious youngster's face.

Her father watched her as she performed these ministrations. He saw the expression in her face as she worked.

'We will take him back with us, Henrietta. He will grow strong and healthy again with plenty of tortilla and beans and good Mexican cooking. Our women will take care of him.'

★　★　★

Some few months later, a tall, powerfully built young man, dressed in stylish Mexican jacket and trousers, walked in a luxuriant garden. Looking diminutive beside his great bulk strolled a young woman.

'Your father has offered me a job as manager over his estates. I do not understand. I have no experience in running a place like this. He would be making a grave mistake to set me up in a position with so great responsibility.'

The girl looked up at the youth. She was extremely attractive.

'Carson, one of my father's talents is that he is a good judge of men. He would not offer you this job if he thought you were not up to it.'

'Still, I have turned him down. I cannot see myself as an overseer.'

He did not see the cloud of dismay flit across her features.

'You turned him down? Don't you see it is a position of trust? Father believes, as do I, that you would be good for our estates.'

Carson shrugged helplessly.

'Perhaps, but I am already committed to the rangers. Now that I am fit again I must return to my old company. I have been promoted.'

He shook his head in genuine bewilderment.

'Why they would do that is a mystery after the mess I made of things over Rodriguez and his band of murderers.'

She put out a hand and grasped the sleeve of his jacket.

'Don't make a decision yet. Think about it for a while.'

'There is nothing to think about. I am a Texas Ranger. That is where my loyalties lie. I must go back.'

'I am sorry to hear you say that. I had hoped you would stay.' Henrietta took a deep breath. 'It was me that asked Father to keep you on.'

Carson stared down at her bowed head.

'I would like you to stay,' she said in a low voice.

Carson looked up from the dark, lustrous hair of the young girl. He knew what she was offering. To stay here was to embrace a life of luxury and ease. He was embarrassed and did not how to reply.

'I must return to the rangers,' he said at last. 'It is the only life I know. It is the only life I am fit for.'

He gestured vaguely at the luxuriant gardens around him.

'I don't fit in here. When I sit at your father's table at the evening meal I feel like a clumsy ox. There is all that crystal and silver knives and spoons and candles and elegant people all babbling away in Spanish and I . . . I know I don't belong.'

She turned a tear-streaked face towards him. He stared in bewilderment at her. Then she was running back up the path.

'Consarn it, Henrietta, I just don't belong,' he muttered to her retreating back.

He looked at the sombrero in his hand and fingered the gold braided straps that adorned it. Then he jammed it on his head and strode purposely towards the stables.

Black Ben eyed up the youngster as he stomped into the corral.

'I take it you told her then?'

'Hell, Ben, I don't fit in here just as much as you don't fit in.'

He looked at the trappers saddled up and waiting for him. Most of them were grinning.

'Why the hell are you all smirking like a pack of jackasses?' he grumbled as he grabbed the bridle of his horse preparatory to mounting.

'Carson,' Middett drawled, 'we gotta long ride back to Texas. I sure as hell hope we don't have to put up with no lovelorn puppy moping along of us.'

Carson's reply was drowned in a gale of laughter from his fellow Texans. Then they were riding out the gate. As Middett observed, it was a long ride back to Texas.

Other titles in the
Linford Western Library:

DESTINATION BOOT HILL

Peter Mallett

Wayne Coulter rode with a gang until an ambush left him wounded, and he might have died if it hadn't been for Henry Mallen and his granddaughter Julie. However, Mallen and Julie are also in trouble, and when Mallen is shot dead, Coulter takes on Julie's enemies. But when a former gang member betrays the outlaws for reward money — it means death. Gun smoke and hot lead will rage in a lethal storm to the very end . . .

TROUBLE AT TAOS

Jackson Davis

Seth Tobin rescued Ruth Simms from Crow attack, thinking that when they reached Fort Union she would be safe living with her Uncle. But as Seth heads for the Rockies, the trader Almedo and the notorious bandit leader Espinosa lust after Ruth. Soon the body count rises as the sound of guns reverberates through the mountains. Can Seth, and the wily old mountain man Dick McGhee, save Ruth from an awful fate — and reap some gold by way of reward . . . ?